Sara. "To be starting out, aiming for something."
Tony pleaded.

"We can't—"

"Do you love me?"

She didn't say it.

He wouldn't make another move until she did.
"Do you?"

He expected his shy Sara to murmur it into his
shirt collar. She pulled back instead. For an instant
he caught her waist in his hands, afraid she'd retreat
altogether. Instead, she looked straight at him, a
resoluteness that bordered on defiance burning in
her eyes. "I never stopped."

His heart swelled with a bittersweet ache. "Then
we can start again. Remember it with me, Sara."

She'd never forgotten. Not the taste of his mouth
nor the feel of his body pressed to hers. He smelled
like spicy aftershave, tangy and real. He smelled like
the pillow she'd hung onto all these months, like a
freshly ironed shirt, the faint scent that was all man.

She recognized the war between gentleness and
passion waging within him, the familiar intensity
that burned in his eyes every time he made her his.
Fear mingled with a curious excitement; her limbs
quivered and her pulse skated erratically through her
veins. She knew what came next—and she wanted it
every bit as much as he did. . . .

WHAT ARE *LOVESWEPT* ROMANCES?

They are stories of true romance and touching emotion. We believe those two very important ingredients are constants in our highly sensual and very believable stories in the LOVESWEPT line. Our goal is to give you, the reader, stories of consistently high quality that may sometimes make you laugh, sometimes make you cry, but are always fresh and creative and contain many delightful surprises within their pages.

Most romance fans read an enormous number of books. Those they truly love, they keep. Others may be traded with friends and soon forgotten. We hope that each LOVESWEPT romance will be a treasure—a "keeper." We will always try to publish

LOVE STORIES YOU'LL NEVER FORGET
BY AUTHORS YOU'LL ALWAYS REMEMBER

The Editors

CLOSE
ENCOUNTERS

TERRY
LAWRENCE

BANTAM BOOKS

NEW YORK · TORONTO · LONDON · SYDNEY · AUCKLAND

CLOSE ENCOUNTERS
A Bantam Book / May 1994

*LOVESWEPT and the wave design are registered
trademarks of Bantam Books, a division of
Bantam Doubleday Dell Publishing Group, Inc.
Registered in U.S. Patent
and Trademark Office and elsewhere.*

*If you would be interested in receiving protective vinyl covers for your
Loveswept books, please write to this address for information:*

*Loveswept
Bantam Books
P.O. Box 985
Hicksville, NY 11802*

ISBN 0-553-44460-3

Published simultaneously in the United States and Canada

*Bantam Books are published by Bantam Books, a division of Bantam Dou-
bleday Dell Publishing Group, Inc. Its trademark, consisting of the words
"Bantam Books" and the portrayal of a rooster, is Registered in U.S. Patent
and Trademark Office and in other countries. Marca Registrada. Bantam
Books, 1540 Broadway, New York, New York 10036.*

PRINTED IN THE UNITED STATES OF AMERICA

OPM   0 9 8 7 6 5 4 3 2 1

ONE

He'd loved Sara from the moment he laid eyes on her eleven years before. Why should the day they signed the divorce papers be any different?

Tony Paretti hesitated at the edge of the hotel lobby and watched as his soon-to-be ex-wife waited for an elevator. He'd get through this day if it killed him. He even had a couple of wisecracks prepared for when the lawyer handed him the pen. *"You want that in ink or in blood?"*

He'd never loved another woman the way he loved Sara Cohen. He probably never would. How many pint-sized intellectual Jewish women, with eyes like big brown chestnuts and hair like knotted silk, would find a lanky Italian sportswriter attractive? She was a tenants' rights activist, concerned, intense, a defender of the weak. He immortalized men who played games for a living, glorifying a world where everything came down to winning and losing.

Losers were the people Sara cared about. Winners were all people wanted to read about in Tony's column. Had something that simple come between them? After a year of torturing himself with whys and what-ifs, he still wasn't sure. Maybe their marriage had been doomed from the start.

He refused to believe it. What they'd had had been too good for too long. Then it all had gone wrong.

Sara moved her scuffed briefcase from one hand to the other. Tony's gut clenched. In front of the banks of elevator doors, she shifted from high heel to high heel. She always chose the height of her shoes in proportion to how intimidated she felt by an opponent. Was that what he'd become to her? He slid a glance down her legs. Stilettos.

They pierced straight to his heart.

He stepped from the carpeted lobby to the marble floor lining the hall of elevators. He elbowed his way through a throng of tourists, bellhops, and office workers. The Joyce Hotel took up the first ten stories of the Cartier Building in downtown Manhattan. The other forty floors contained offices, including a hive of lawyers on the top three. He and Sara would shake hands in one of those offices, polite, resigned, solemn. Saying hello now would only prolong their parting. Tony stepped up behind her. "Sara?"

She didn't hear. A bell pinged and a white triangle lit above the elevator doors. Bodies surged out. The waiting crowd parted, then pushed forward. A bellboy with a luggage rack took up half the available space. Despite her petite size, Sara couldn't squeeze in. Tony watched her shoulders slump as she sighed and the doors closed.

She scanned the brass plaque with the rows of illuminated numbers displaying where each elevator stopped. Of twelve cars in transit, only two were heading down toward the first floor.

Faces raised, people watched numbers climb up the plaque the way a baseball crowd follows a long line drive into the bleachers. "In Vegas they'd take bets on which elevator would reach the top first," Tony quipped to no one in particular.

Grinning, a middle-aged man agreed. "You got that right."

This time Sara heard. Tony watched her shoulders rise as tension crept up her back. In another day and time he would have reached out and massaged those shoulders gently. "How ya doin', babe?" he would have whispered in her ear. Whoever she was off to do battle with, he would have supported her.

Damn him if he didn't want to make this easy on her too.

He kept his hands at his sides, relieved she hadn't turned around. It gave him a moment to gather himself. "She wants this," he thought. For the hundredth time he promised himself he'd bow out manfully. He wouldn't beg, make scenes, shout—all of which he'd done a year ago when the pain and shock of her request were still fresh.

Marriage was a two-way street; this had to be half his fault. But there'd be plenty of time for Monday-morning quarterbacking the next day. And the day after that. And all the nights.

He caught a whiff of her perfume. Sucking in a deep breath, he felt that familiar empty sensation near his heart. "Aren't you going to say hello?"

Heads turned. People glanced hurriedly, then looked away. Tony waited for Sara to arrange her expression into a polite mask. He'd loved her for eleven years. He ought to know what went through her head by now.

She surprised him. When she turned, her smile was tender, almost sorry. "I wasn't sure you'd come."

"I said I would." Pushing the words past the lump in his throat made them come out harsh.

Her eyes clouded. She looked away, tucking her briefcase under her arm, clamping it beside her heart.

A bell pinged overhead. They squeezed into the elevator with a dozen other people. A matronly woman with a bulging shopping bag wedged between Tony and Sara. Everyone faced front. Voices declared their destinations. The doors closed. The elevator began its journey toward the fiftieth floor.

Tony stared at the top of Sara's head. Sometimes the clock ran out, he thought. The inning ended, the shot didn't go in, the Hail Mary pass sailed over the receiver's outstretched hands. He'd always been the one to sit down after the game and say exactly what went wrong, where the momentum was lost, the crucial play fumbled.

For the life of him, he couldn't say what had gone wrong with them. They'd talked it out until they couldn't talk anymore. Then they'd separated. She'd filed.

Part of him still couldn't accept that it was over. Details nagged at him. He'd seen something outside the elevator, something in the way she'd come prepared: briefcase for armor, shoes for height, a pin-striped power suit with a low-necked silk blouse beneath it. The cameo on her lapel clinched it. Her mother had given it to her in grade school when she won her first spelling bee. She wore it when she needed reassurance.

Did that mean she still loved him? Or was he clutching at straws? Sara was a dynamo of preparedness, a writer of lists and itineraries. Was she less than ready to cut him from her life?

He jangled the coins in his pocket, brushing his thumb over the raised surface of the St. Jude medal his mother had pressed into his hand over the breakfast table that morning. "Take this," she'd said.

"The patron saint of lost causes?"

His mother dabbed her nose with her apron. "Talk to her," she commanded in heavily accented English. "Talk to her before it's too late."

"God knows I've tried, Ma."

"You love this girl."

"God knows that too."

Watching the numbers rise on the elevator panel, Tony pressed the medal between his thumb and forefinger until he felt the impression on his skin. Cameos, medals—maybe he was as superstitious as Sara. Maybe a little divine intervention was all they needed. God knew, nothing else had worked.

The car stopped at the fifth floor, then the ninth. Four hotel guests got off, tiredly shoving their luggage before them. The people in the elevator took advantage of the extra room to exhale and shift their weight. Tony shouldered his way between several men in suits until he was behind Sara.

The elevator lifted off. Their heels pressed into the carpet until their bodies adjusted to the upward motion. His body swayed, barely touching hers. He sensed her teeter on her heels. The leather briefcase creaked as she squeezed it. He took that as a good sign. Piped-in music filled the air. So did someone's perfume.

Tony cleared his throat. "How's my soon-to-be ex-wife?"

Heads turned ever so slightly.

"Fine." Eyes front, Sara pressed her lips together.

"Fine," he repeated, a touch sarcastically. "Got the papers in there?"

She released the death grip on her briefcase. Sliding it from beneath her arm, she held the handle in front of her with both hands. The movement of the car bounced it lightly against her knees.

Only Tony noticed her locked elbows. A golf coach would have a lot to say about that tense grip.

"I told you I'd mail you the papers," she said, her voice deliberately low.

"I wanted to be here," he replied in a conversational tone everyone picked up plainly. "I attended the wedding. The least I can do is attend the divorce."

One man huffed. A woman cleared her throat daintily, casting Tony a sympathetic glance. He smiled faintly. He could almost hear Sara's silent protest: *Everyone's listening*. Peeking over her shoulder, he watched her cheeks flush.

She twisted her chin around and glared at him, daring their audience to listen in. "You didn't contest it."

He felt the crowd's sympathy shift. Advantage Sara.

The elevator slowed at fourteen. His heels lifted slightly off the ground. Two women in front got off. As they turned down the hall, they snuck a glance at the intriguing couple, their whispered conclusions lost in the whoosh of the closing doors. The elevator headed toward sixteen.

Tony breathed a sigh of relief. Luck had put them on a nonexpress. But the next button lit was for the twenty-fifth floor. They'd be at fifty in no time. At twenty-five he used the jostle of two exiting riders to step around Sara.

A single passenger came on board. "Twenty-nine," he said.

Tony graciously pushed twenty-nine. And thirty-one. And thirty-four. If a year's separation hadn't solved their problems, the few extra minutes gained might not matter. He'd take any chance he could get. Discreetly nudging the control panel with his elbow, he lit more stops than there were passengers.

He stepped coolly back to Sara. The center of avid attention, they stood shoulder to shoulder in the middle of the car. "About time we got this taken care of," he began. "Sign the papers. Move on. From what I hear, you've enjoyed our year of separation. Or is the dating game less than it's cracked up to be?"

She knew exactly what he was doing. "Don't start this, Tony."

"Don't stop it, Sara."

The elevator paused again. Two businessmen practically leapt to safety. The doors closed on the hushed attention of five remaining souls.

"Your mother thought we—"

"I don't care what other people think," Sara exploded.

"I do. I want to talk about this."

"We've talked and talked. It's too late, Tony."

"Is it?" Before he knew what came over him, he stepped forward and pushed every button between thirty-five and fifty. "Now we can talk."

People moaned. Voices erupted. "What do you think you're doing?" "I have an appointment." "I need to be on forty-one by one o'clock."

Tony swung around to face the throng. "Sorry, folks. I need to talk to my wife."

A livid Englishman in a bowler hat took charge of the mutiny, repeatedly pressing the button for the forty-seventh floor. It did nothing to diminish the glow of the intervening numbers. "Really!"

Curses flew. The doors opened at the next floor, and the next. The ball was in Tony's court. By thirty-six, he knew what to say. "I love you, Sara."

She looked at him, her cheeks aflame, her big brown eyes glistening. "Tough."

He grinned, pressing the shoulder of his rumpled suit against the wall. "You know I love it when you stand up to me."

She squared her shoulders, aware of the resentful stares of people trapped in a boxing match with nothing to look forward to but the counterpunch. "Double tough."

Disappointed sighs met her weak comeback. Tony shook his head. "Come on, Sara, your vocabulary's bigger than that. You've used some of it on me. Heck, I taught you some of it. Go ahead. Argue with me, hit me, hate me." The bravado died as quickly as it had come. He couldn't kid about this forever. He reached out, tilting her chin up. "Whatever you do, just don't leave me out in the cold this way."

She wrenched her chin away. Striding to the far corner, she wedged herself between two businessmen. She dropped the briefcase beside her calf and rested her hand on the brass railing. Her posture was perfect, her poise imperturbable. Only Tony glimpsed the flash of white as her knuckles gripped the rail.

The elevator stopped at thirty-eight. An outraged rider got off at the last second, having almost forgotten his stop. Tony looked balefully at a secretary perched on the threshold waiting to enter. "Believe me, you don't want on."

Speechless, the woman clutched her file folders to her chest as the doors slid shut.

They stopped at two more floors, the air thick with tension.

"Take him back," a voice said at last.

Sara's head snapped around.

"Yeah, take him back so we can get out of here," someone else grumbled.

"Tell him ya love him and let's go."

"New Yorkers." Tony grinned. "Is there a greater bunch of people anywhere else on Earth?" It was a cheap play for civic pride, but he had the people on his side again.

Sara folded her arms and stared at the closing doors.

Tony thought his way past a couple more stops as the doors opened on empty corridors. He wasn't a planner like Sara. He spoke from the gut. He fell back on a no-fail halftime rouser courtesy of

Vince Lombardi. "As someone once said, 'Loving isn't everything, it's the only thing.' "

"That's winning," she replied tartly.

"I don't want to lose you. If we walk away now, we both lose."

"The sportswriter speaks. This isn't a game, Tony."

"It's my life. It's yours—"

"Tony?" A balding man in a leather jacket piped up. "Are you Tony Paretti of the *Daily News*? *That* Tony Paretti?"

Tony nodded, his frustrated gaze fixed on Sara's. She sighed and looked away.

"You were great, man. When Steinbrenner got canned— And that article about Montana's come-back— What did ya go to that paper in Pittsburgh for?"

"Chicago."

"Whatever. There's no teams like New York teams. Man, we got the Jets, the Nets, the Mets, the—" Ping.

"Your floor?" Tony asked.

The man reluctantly sidled his way out of the car, but not before giving Tony a punch on the arm. "The city lost a good writer the day it lost you. Hey lady, mark my words. He's a keeper."

The doors closed. The elevator lurched and rose one more floor.

"At least *he* likes me," Tony said.

"Then he can marry you."

"He thinks you should come back to me. So does everyone else here."

Nods outnumbered grumbles.

"I don't care what other people think!"

"Funny. I remember you saying that the day I proposed." He turned to the matronly woman. "I'm Catholic, she's Jewish," he explained helpfully.

"Ah." The woman eyed Sara a little more closely.

"There was some concern among our families—"

"What does she care about our families?" Sara wailed. "This is ridiculous. You're airing our dirty laundry in public *again*."

The woman patted Sara's arm. "There's nothing to be ashamed of. Mixed marriages are tricky. Take my nephew. Married a Chinese girl. You would've thought—" Ping. "Oh dear. This is my floor." She stepped over the threshold, taking her perfume and her shopping bag with her. As the doors closed she winked at Sara before turning to Tony. "He's trying, honey. If I don't see you again, *mazel tov*."

"Ciao." Tony waved. Making instant friends was a talent of his. So was driving Sara up the wall.

"That's all I need, an elevator yenta," she muttered.

The doors shut completely, then bounced against each other and opened halfway. Everyone faced front as if expecting another pronouncement from the departed matchmaker. No one was there. At last the doors wobbled closed, hushed and hesitant, and the elevator lifted off.

"False alarm," Tony said.

"If you insist on accosting me, I'll ring the real alarm," Sara snapped.

"It's symbolic. One door closes, another opens."

"Five more floors, Tony."

"You would think that way."

"What does that mean?"

"You know what it means."

The remaining riders shifted nervously. Two out of three muttered about getting off next. The bowler-hatted Englishman stabbed the button for forty-seven with the tip of his umbrella.

"What I mean," Tony growled, "was how you keep track of everything. You're probably counting the minutes until you get rid of me. You know where you're going for dinner after you sign the papers, how soon you'll sell the apartment, for how much, what your budget will be."

"I knew that—" She bit her tongue.

Tony stood up straight, posture rigid as he completed the sentence for her. "You knew that before I even moved out."

The elevator stopped again, its passengers frozen in place. No one met Sara's gaze. She faced Tony alone. "I needed to know how I'd make the payments. I'm responsible about managing money. Unlike some people."

"I was never broke."

"You were close."

"I can handle money just fine."

"Manhandle it, you mean. You toss it around the way—the way your mother dishes out pasta. Tips, cab fares, extravagant presents."

They'd reached forty-seven, but the doors only opened an inch. Using his umbrella as a crowbar, the man in the bowler hat pried them apart.

"Stop that," Tony commanded. "We aren't going anywhere."

"I'll say!"

With a whoosh like a dying sigh, the doors opened a foot. The man forced them apart as if he were Samson and squeaked through. He turned and tipped his hat, veins popping out on his forehead. "Good day!"

"Thanks for the *lift*," Tony called.

"We better get out of here too," the last two riders declared. One held the doors open as the other hopped out. For the first time Tony noticed the elevator had stopped a good six inches below floor level.

He barely cared. He turned to Sara, his fists clenched in his pockets, his stomach knotted. He forced a smile onto his face. "Alone at last."

The doors opened before she could reply. Still on forty-seven.

"I hope that doesn't happen for every time he hit the button," Tony muttered. "This is where we're going, right?" His finger hovered over fifty. He didn't push it. This had been his last chance to talk to her, and he'd messed it up the way he had every other one. "Sara, I'm sorry. Is there any way—"

She bent and picked up her briefcase, ready to depart. Tony sighed and pushed the button.

The elevator hummed and began moving. Sara stared at the numbers on the panel above the door, forty-eight, forty-nine. Her eyes filled with tears. Tony wanted to go to her. He couldn't. Pride, stubbornness, fear, just plain pain stopped him where he stood. The elevator shuddered to a halt.

"I'm sorry, babe. But what can I do? I've said everything I know how to say. Talk to me. Princess?"

One corner of her mouth crooked in a hopeless smile. He knew she hated that nickname. An only child of much older parents, she'd been cherished and pampered. Nevertheless, she'd worked hard in return, earning their love, excelling at everything and making it look easy. To those who didn't know her, the name Princess might fit perfectly.

Tony saw below the well-prepared surface. Amid all his teasing, she'd never know how sincerely he meant that nickname, how proud he was of everything she'd accomplished, with and without him.

Maybe that was their problem. To him, she *was* a princess, and he was the luckiest footman alive. "Is this my fault?" he asked.

She refused to meet his gaze. "Thanks for making a fool of me in front of all those people," she croaked.

He shrugged, gripping the St. Jude medal in his pocket. "Ten years of marriage—"

"—lets you know a person's weaknesses. You know I hate being embarrassed. That was rotten."

"All's fair, as they say."

"That only applies in war and hockey games."

He barked a laugh. "Mind if I use that in my column?"

"Do they play hockey in Chicago?"

He rolled his eyes. "For the wife of a sportswriter—"

"Soon to be ex-wife." She ran her fingers through her hair, trying to comb back a twisted strand of frizz. "Push the button, Tony. We can't talk here."

"If we don't talk now—"

"We couldn't talk at all. That's why we broke up. I can't stay married to someone I can't talk to." Her eyes met his and brimmed. "Please?"

Ten years of marriage and he still couldn't resist her. He pushed fifty. His gut wrenched. So did the elevator. The lights on the panel flickered between forty-nine and fifty.

She sniffed, dabbing the tip of her nose with the back of her hand. She gradually became aware they weren't moving. "Why isn't anything happening?" she asked suspiciously.

He shrugged and pushed the button again.

"Let me do it." She strode to the panel.

"You don't trust me?"

"Should I?"

Any other time he would have smiled at her brass. Any other time he would have told her how much he loved her.

Before he could get the words out, she'd pushed fifty with a no-nonsense jab. The doors opened. The elevator lurched up, then down. The forty-ninth floor was suddenly a foot higher than the elevator floor.

"Tony?" She edged backward, her gaze meeting his as the doors shut with a bang. The car plunged down the shaft.

TWO

The brakes screeched, their high-pitched whine sharpening as the elevator slid downward. Sara screamed and rushed into Tony's arms.

He crushed her to his chest. Not now, he thought. How many times had he prayed to hold his wife one more time? Every detail was fixed in his brain. Her fingers curled in his lapels, her face hidden against the side of his neck. "I love you," he shouted, his voice harsh over a hammering heart.

He could have sworn he heard her say "I love you" back.

Time stretched into an eternity, then snapped like a rubber band. The screeching brakes held. They jerked to a halt.

Tony and Sara listened together, their breath stopped, their heartbeats held in check, straining to sense whether the elevator had truly stopped or whether they were falling through space. They looked at the lighted panel. Thirty-nine and holding.

Sara kept her voice soft for fear a loud noise might dislodge them. "We fell ten floors?"

"We didn't fall," he said. "It slipped."

"Is that all." Her voice failed her. Humor failed her. The only thing holding her up was Tony. She'd always known he would step between her and death itself if he had to. But he hadn't been there the rest of the time, when she'd needed him most. When it came to the feelings she most needed to express, he'd walled her out.

She banished the familiar blame and clung to him, snatching a few more precious seconds, relishing the good things they'd had. If only it could be that way again, the hurts pared away, love stripped to its core.

She cherished the details, the smell of his skin, the faint stubble on the side of his neck. Everything about Tony was immediate. In his presence, their year apart evaporated like a mist. But the graphic physical reality also emphasized the emotional abyss between them. Sooner or later she'd have to let go, to step away and pretend none of this had happened, to forget she'd ever blurted out the words "I love you."

The fact they were true didn't matter a whit. She couldn't go back to their marriage because he held her in a crisis. He'd wanted the divorce, she reminded herself. He'd barely contested it. He was so eager to sign the papers, he'd flown in from Chicago for the big day.

She withdrew from his arms, dimly aware of the way he held her waist a moment longer. Then he let go.

Her knees shook badly. She barely trusted the stiletto heels to support her until she reached the corner. Safely there, she leaned against the railing, her nerves frayed, her lungs aching. Her thoughts returned to their present crisis. At least it spared them exploring the emotional minefield of their tattered relationship.

She considered every angle of their predicament, starting with the worst-case scenario. "The brakes could still fail, couldn't they?"

"They won't."

"How do you know?"

"They're locked. They held."

The way he'd held her? She'd once thought that was a sure thing too. She looked away.

Tony pressed his back against the far corner, his hands spread on the rail. They were like boxers in a ring, she thought, separated by the referee for holding, merely retreating to their corners before the second round.

She braced herself for the familiar ache of exhaustion. A year ago she couldn't have borne another round. She'd been so tired of talking, pleading, watching every argument dig the ruts deeper.

She closed her eyes and waited for the worst of the pain to wash over her. It didn't come. For a year she'd survived by remembering what drove them apart; recalling the good times hurt too much. Touching Tony had brought them flooding back. Unbidden memories, raw, stunning, intense, threatened to overwhelm her resolve.

She'd made her plans. Concentrating on details would get her through this. Letting her heart founder in old emotions wouldn't. She wasn't here to hurt him. Only leave him.

Loving him was another matter entirely. She studied his face. Breathing heavily, he dragged a hand over his mouth. She sensed the adrenaline pumping through him by the depth of the lines etched beside his mouth. The body she'd touched seemed leaner, bullwhip taut. Had he lost weight? Had he dreaded this day the way she had?

He'd said he loved her. In his way he probably did. With Tony common sense took a backseat to tumultuous, unpredictable emotions. He was all heart. She needed more. She needed talk, words, to examine their relationship and *know* it was on stable ground. If love alone could have solved their problems, she'd be in his arms right now. She wouldn't be hugging herself with trembling hands. He wouldn't be standing there staring back at her, a bleak smile on his narrow lips.

Faint purple smudges outlined his eyes. Eyes the color of melting chocolate, Sara thought. She'd seen them crinkle with laughter and pool with tears. But he'd never cried when it mattered most. When it had mattered, he'd walked away.

Her gaze faltered, focusing on his long, narrow hands as he yanked the knot in his tie and roughly unbuttoned his collar button. He shrugged inside a jacket her clenched fists had tugged awry. She blamed his nervous activity on the elevator's plunge, once again aware of the flutter in her veins.

Head back, she took a deep breath, examining the ceiling. It wasn't fear skittering through her in tiny electric shocks. Her palms itched from the scratch of his wool sport coat, exiled from his touch. Her lungs felt hollow, her breasts heavy. She couldn't go on wanting him this way. She had to move on with her life.

She reviewed her resolutions for getting through this day in a detached, businesslike manner. *They'd tried everything. They couldn't go on. He wanted this.* It all sounded as hollow as she felt.

Tony turned to the panel, scanning the buttons with a frown.

Sara folded her arms across her waist. "Should we try again?"

His head snapped around. His mouth twisted in a pained smile. "You think we should?"

She felt her cheeks color and deliberately kept her gaze on the control panel. "I meant push the button."

"I guessed that."

She hated hurting him. She'd filed to spare them this. At the time it seemed like the only way out. *Irreconcilable differences.*

His finger hovered over the button. "You know, this could be the end of it."

One way or the other. She swallowed.

"Say when."

"Give me a minute." She snatched up her briefcase, pawing through the purse section to fetch a lipstick. The lid snapped off with a snick. She turned to one of the mirrored walls, forcing her hand to stop shaking while she outlined bow-shaped lips.

"Lipstick? Now?"

She refused to meet his gaze in the mirror. She knew that tone, tolerant, affectionate, teasing. Long-married, she thought, her throat closing up again. "You know I like to be prepared."

He knew her better than anyone. She couldn't ever imagine letting another man get that close to her, couldn't imagine telling someone else all the secrets Tony knew, revealing all her faults. He loved her in spite of them. She found a brush and fluffed the tight curls that fell in a wavy slant across the left side of her forehead. "I read somewhere that cruise ship mirrors were tinted pink so seasick passengers would think they looked healthy."

"Yeah?"

Chitchat. Was that all she could muster? They could have died in each other's arms just then. But they couldn't live with each other. For the hundredth time she reminded herself of that.

He cocked a thumb toward the panel. "Is anything better than staying here with me?"

"I didn't say that."

"You didn't have to." He ran his hand up the walnut paneling surrounding the brass plaque. "I heard what you did say." He meant the "I love you."

Her heart stumbled. Her defenses rose. Damn him for being so calm and collected. She *knew* him. She knew when he hurt and when he was too damn proud to show it. Did he think she couldn't see how his fist clenched in his pocket, how his gaze shied from hers? A grimace tightened below his right eye whenever he looked directly at her, like a flinch.

She shoved the brush back in her briefcase. Maybe she flattered herself more than the tinted mirrors. Maybe he was angry, fed up. Maybe his thumb hovered over that button because he wanted out as badly as she did. "Go," she said.

"You really want to go through with this?"

She hugged the case to her. He'd never know about the nights she'd slept with his pillow clutched to her, resting her cheek on an imaginary chest. As if presenting a case before an unsympathetic judge, she pretended more confidence than she felt. "Go."

He pushed the button. Invisible cams whirred.

Sara and Tony braced themselves. Nothing happened. The car didn't plunge or rise. Tony slicked back his hair with both hands and sighed. "Try again?" he asked over his shoulder.

If only they could.

He turned as if she'd spoken. She glared at the panel and nodded.

Nothing. "I'm going to try Door Open." He punched the button with his thumb.

"That's Door Close."

"No, it isn't." He pressed it twice for good measure.

"When the arrows point in, that means Door Close."

"Why don't they just write Close on it so people can read it?"

"Because not everyone can read. Including some of your multimillionaire sports stars."

"Don't give me the underprivileged-and-exploited speech."

"I'm just saying the buttons are international symbols."

"Then why do they confuse *me* every time?"

She stifled a grin and shrugged. "Don't look at me."

He did, canting his head toward the panel. "Symbols in this building are false advertising. Anybody who comes in here better be able to read the fine print."

Her chin tilted up. He'd known it would.

"Is that a crack about lawyers?"

"Why not?"

"Go ahead, insult my profession."

"It's lawyers who got us here, isn't it?"

"Push the button."

He grinned. "I think I just did."

She wrestled with a grin of her own. He loved rubbing her the wrong way and watching her bristle. And she fell for it every time. Once upon a time she would have taken the teasing in stride. "Once upon a time" was how fairy tales began. He caught her frown and turned back to the panel. "I take it Door Open is the one with the arrows going that way?"

"Correct."

He planted his thumb on it. The doors sighed, stuttered, moved apart six inches, then stopped altogether.

Patience, Sara thought. After all the effort it took to fortify herself for their meeting, a stuck elevator was a temporary glitch. A new scenario popped into her head. "What if they don't open?"

"Give me a chance."

"We'll be trapped."

"You've never been claustrophobic before."

"No." She drew the word out doubtfully. "We've never been trapped in an elevator before."

"I've been married to you for ten years, *cara*, you'll be fine."

Cara, the Italian word for dear heart. She hadn't heard that word in twelve months.

Tony caught the doubts in her eyes, pain and memory twining like barbs twisted around wire. She didn't trust him.

He roughly pushed the pain aside. They didn't have many options in a stalled elevator. Shoving his hands in his pockets, he strolled to her side of the car. All he wanted to do was reassure her, get the fear out of her eyes. A little leftover love had to be good for something. "We aren't trapped, *cara*. Somebody, something, has given us one more chance to talk."

She crooked a spare-me smile. He remembered her disdain for his romantic streak. She didn't trust nebulous concepts like fate, destiny, love that lasts forever. He'd staked his life on them the day he said "for better or worse."

Things couldn't get much worse.

"No more talk," she said.

"You used to insist we talk more."

"Look where it got us."

"Now I'm arguing for more and you for less. Ironic, huh?"

"Just say 'I told you so' and we'll leave it at that."

"Uh-uh." Loving her was an issue he had to prove. Keeping her was the only way he knew how to do it. He scanned the five-foot-by-seven-foot space. "If talking doesn't work, maybe other things will. There is something we haven't tried."

She glanced at the deep blue carpet with its light gray flecks. Her eyes widened as she caught his meaning. "Don't be silly."

He angled his body closer, careful not to frighten her, needing desperately to draw her in. "This never failed. When words failed we could always apologize like this, Sara. Touch like this. Kiss and make up. Like this."

Her gaze fastened on his lips. "That's no way to solve an argument."

"It's the best way to show love. Sometimes it's the only way."

He closed the distance. Her lids lowered, but her body remained watchful and alert. "Words—"

she began, her lips unconsciously molded into the perfect shape for a kiss.

"Let your lips tell me what you want to say, *cara*. Talk to me." He kissed her gently, his lips catching slightly on her newly applied lipstick, brushing air-soft over her mouth. "Don't close me out, Sara. Please."

Frustration urged him to do more. Rare caution held him back. The kiss rocked him, the emptiness that had haunted him since their breakup threatened to swamp him. He wanted to be married to her. He'd never stopped being married to her. She made his life complete—and this was the only way he knew how to tell her.

The tip of his tongue tasted the waxy red shade she wore. He waited, wondering if too much had happened, if too much time had passed. It couldn't be too late. "Sara." He raised his hands, cupping her shoulders, urging her to him.

She tasted good, real. Hunger welled in him, fueled by a year of futile dreams and bitter recriminations, a year of hotel rooms and road trips and telephones he hadn't had the guts to pick up and use. *Sara*.

He lifted his head, breaking the kiss, silently begging her to stay. Her breath feathered across his chin. She didn't move. He shut his eyes tight against the pain. His logical, determined, coolheaded Sara had to come to him. She had to. He rested his forehead on hers for a second. Dredging up courage he'd never known he had, he tried one last time.

His lips touched hers, parted and pressed. He waited. The tip of her tongue, warm and wet, trembled and touched his. He felt it as if it were an electric shock. Emotions he couldn't name shot through him. He tilted his head, careful and slow, his tongue exploring the raspy velvet of hers, the sweet liquid heat he knew so well.

The shrill scream of the alarm bell jolted them apart.

Tony cursed and spun toward the door. He immediately turned back. Too late. She'd retreated, turning hurriedly to the mirror to press her lips together and smooth her mussed lipstick. She finger-combed her hair with shaking hands. Ready for rescue. Ready to meet the lawyers and go through with it.

With a black curse, Tony strode to the panel and pushed the answering alarm with three long blasts. S. O. S.

Someone repeated the signal in answering rings. A voice shouted from outside the car. "Are you stuck?"

"Hell, yes, we're stuck," Tony boomed.

Sara covered her ears, scolding him with a frown.

"Can you open the doors?" the voice yelled. The empty shaft surrounding them created a distant echo.

Tony hesitated over the two Door buttons, then hit the correct one. The doors parted, revealing a dismal wall of chalky mortar and ancient red bricks.

"Elevator doors aren't supposed to do that," Sara insisted. "I read it somewhere."

"Elevators aren't supposed to drop ten floors, either."

Sara retreated until the brass rail bumped her lower back. Her nostrils constricted at the smell of greased cables. Her stomach clenched at the stench of burned rubber. The brakes were locked and holding, she reminded herself fiercely. Tony had said so. She pictured the vast emptiness where their elevator dangled. Sounds of other elevators hummed past them. "Are we the only ones who are stuck?" she asked him.

"We'll find out."

A man's voice, much louder and tinged with a Jamaican accent, echoed down the chamber. "We get you out soon as we can, mon."

"Sooner," Tony demanded. Brooking no argument, he took Sara's hand in his. "Get this thing moving. My wife's claustrophobic."

"That's not exactly true," Sara demurred.

He squeezed her hand and shrugged. "Whatever works."

Feeling suddenly, implausibly safe, she lost a battle with her resolve and looked directly in his eyes. "You're a devil, you know that?"

Brown eyes darkened over a cautiously cocky grin. "I had the feeling I was about to find out."

Her mouth grew dry. She moistened her lips. "Tony—"

A second voice yelled, this one steeped in Brooklynese. "Hey Mac, what floor you on?"

Tony stepped into the opened doorway, fingertips splayed on the brick wall for balance. He looked up through the slit.

Sara let his other hand go, glancing prudently downward. She wasn't getting anywhere near that pitch-black four-inch space between the doorsill and the wall.

"We're between floors," Tony shouted upward.

"All de floors are numbered. On de bottom and sides."

"There are bricks and cement and that's it," Tony replied.

Sara edged forward. Keeping her pointed heels well back from the slotted sill, she shouted upward too. "The number panel reads thirty-nine."

"Thirty-nine?" Brooklyn asked.

Was it her imagination or did he sound troubled by that? The ensuing silence wasn't reassuring.

Steadying her, Tony cupped her elbow in his palm. She grew bolder. He'd always had that effect on her, urging her to greater heights, luring her out of a safely contained world that would have suffocated her without his breezy air of bravado and risk.

She caught a glimpse of the darkness above. "Thirty-nine," she repeated loudly. "Of course, it might be wrong. The elevator *is* broken."

Tony laughed, a husky whisper. "I always did love that dry sense of humor."

She shook off the shivery sensation of his breath on her cheek, determined to resist his charm. "I was just being logical."

"That's something else I always loved."

"Shush."

A murmured consultation continued above. The sound of male voices fell toward them like the ripples of a waterfall. Minutes dragged by. Sara stepped back to the center of the car, thinking. Yes, he'd said he loved her. But marriage involved more than love. She needed trust, constancy, communication. "I love you" didn't answer the questions she needed answered most. A kiss could be a kiss good-bye.

They'd be rescued at any moment. They'd go to Melchior's office. If Tony signed the papers, she'd have her answer in black and white. Some differences were irreconcilable.

If he signed, she'd survive. She had a schedule

to stick to, a life to get back on track. She'd had enough havoc for one day. Their present mechanical failure was simply a perfect example of a miserable day getting more miserable by the minute.

Determined to face the worst head-on, she stepped up to the open doors, evading Tony's outstretched hand. "Look, we have an appointment," she called.

"Speak for yourself, sister."

To her immense surprise, Tony shouldered her back inside.

"Take all the time you need," he yelled up the shaft.

"But we're trapped!"

He gave her his most maddeningly carefree shrug. "What's the point in panicking? Going anywhere?"

She glared at the bricks. "That's pretty funny coming from someone who's already picked up and moved to Chicago. I happened to have plans for today."

"So life decided to take a U-turn. You don't like it, take it up with the man upstairs." His pointed finger implied someone even higher up than their conferring repairmen.

"Those probably aren't even repairmen," she muttered. "They're probably janitors. Handymen."

"They came in handy today."

"Don't get cute. Get us out of here!" She winced at her shrill tone bouncing back at her from the bricks.

"How many of you are there?" Brooklyn called.

"Two!"

"What're your names?"

"Sara Cohen."

"And Tony Paretti."

"*The* Tony Paretti?" the Jamaican said.

"Oh, great." Sara moaned.

"Yep," Tony replied, his grin spreading.

Sara knew he couldn't help it; the man had an ego the size of North Dakota. And a smile known to stop traffic and women's hearts, hers in particular. She retreated to her corner.

Tony chuckled as the words "*Daily News*," "sportswriter," and "championship" floated down to them, one rescuer explaining their guest's importance to the other. "And they say no one reads newspapers anymore," Tony quipped.

With a sigh, Sara rested her forehead against the mirrored glass. "They forgot the part about the Pulitzer."

"I read you all the time, mon," Jamaica shouted down.

"Thank you," Tony called.

Brooklyn broke in. "Remember the series on big-time betting on college games?"

The Pulitzer prize piece. Tony cocked a brow in Sara's direction. She drew one point in the air.

"Look, you guys, what're your names?" he shouted.

"DuWayne."

"Roberto."

"Roberto and DuWayne, can you fix this thing?"

"Not right now, Mr. Paretti. We do wiring, not elevators."

"We had a complaint about the car stopping all the time. Thought we'd check it out."

"See?" Sara hissed. "All the people who got off complained about *us*."

"The door, she don't work right," Roberto explained. "But don't you worry 'bout a t'ing. We get you fixed right soon."

In a flash Sara shoved Tony aside. "I need you to contact Mr. Melchior. Michael Melchior. We had an appointment with him at one-thirty."

"You two together?"

"Not for long," Tony muttered.

"He's on the fiftieth floor," Sara shouted.

"Okey-dokey. De engineer is on his way. Maybe an hour more."

"He fixed this baby last month," DuWayne put in. "Knows all about how it works."

Sara threw up her hands. "Wonderful! It's been repaired before."

"And will be again," Tony responded reasonably.

She ignored his outstretched palm and the comforting look that went with it, pacing back to her corner.

"Hey, mon, DuWayne has a question he too shy to ask."

Tony squinted at Sara's back, guessing exactly what was coming. "Go ahead."

"Who're you picking for the Super Bowl?"

"The Broncos."

DuWayne's voice rose an octave. "Broncos?! No way."

"Sit tight, mon. Be back soon." The whoosh of a closing door smothered the rest of their debate.

"Sports," Sara spat out, "the opiate of the masculine masses."

They listened to the silence. Sara paced from corner to corner along the back wall. One, two, three, turn.

Tony watched her reflection in the mirrors, hundreds of them receding in infinity, the two of them separated as far as the eye could see. He turned to his right, reached out, and touched brick and jagged cement, cold as a headstone.

"Don't," she said.

He dropped a glance to the black slit between the car and the wall. "I can't fall through that."

Sara rubbed both arms, chilled by the cold seeping off the bricks. "Just close the door, please."

Tony pressed Door Close. Each side slid inward, bounced back, then closed with a dull thud. He turned to his wife. "Alone at last."

THREE

The sense of utter privacy settled around them like a blanket. Silence enveloped them. With the brass doors closed, the elevator took on a cozy, intimate feel. Or so Tony thought as he examined their snug space. It amazed him how much effort it took not to close the distance between him and Sara in two quick strides. "Nice place," he quipped.

"Mm."

Faint swirls gave a brushed finish to the brass doors. Soft light glowed from a ledge around the ceiling, spilling warmly over the gold-tinged mirrors. The brass rail and the walnut paneling below it reminded him of a private corner in some old English pub. Plush blue carpet absorbed the distant whir of the other elevators going by, other people on their way places.

Like lawyers' offices.

He frowned at the thought. In a space five feet deep by seven feet wide, he suddenly had no idea where to look or stand. Years ago he'd have known. He'd have taken Sara in his arms as naturally as the grass grew in Fenway Park. He'd have told her everything was going to be all right. Right then he had no guarantees to give. Fate had given him an hour at the most to repair their crumbled marriage. Sara's response to his kiss had given him the nutty notion he could win her back, given time.

"You think we'll run out of air?" she asked.

They'd run out of time first.

Getting no answer from him, Sara made herself at home. She stood her briefcase in the corner and perched her petite rear end on it. Elbows on her knees, she sank her chin in one hand.

Fifty-nine minutes and counting, Tony thought. For all their bickering, he hadn't gotten any of the answers he'd thought he needed when he arrived that morning. It was time he started asking. "I want to know what went wrong."

Her brows rose as if that were the dumbest question she'd ever heard. "Who cares? They fix it; we go home."

"I'm talking about us."

He would have accepted her helpless shrug as an answer if it hadn't been for the flash of pain in her eyes, as bleak as the wintry New York day outside.

At last she spoke up. "If that could have been fixed, we wouldn't be here."

"In this fix, you mean?"

She groaned. "Tony, please."

His usual cocky smile didn't work. "Sorry. Wanted to get that gloom and doom out of your eyes."

"Everything will work out somehow."

In a million years she'd never get him used to the idea of living without her. No matter how kind and caring she was about dumping him. "You're comforting *me* now?"

"People survive divorce all the time."

"I don't want survival. I want to live, really live. With you. *Cara*—" He should have known he couldn't keep the passion out of his voice, couldn't stay on his side of the elevator.

She stood, stopping him in his tracks. Kicked over, the briefcase thudded against the back wall. Sara's arms wrapped around her middle. Her stricken gaze fell to the dark blue carpet, rising only to communicate that crazy combination of pain disguised as encouragement. "We tried. It didn't work, okay? This happens. People marry too young, they make mistakes—"

"They stop communicating?"

"We talked constantly."

"Until the going got rough, then we couldn't keep it up."

"Exactly." She looked him right in the eye, the way she did when she was making a case against an adversary in court. "We had to stop hurting each other. There was nothing more to say."

Hence the separation. The filing. She was doing this to help him. It was for his own good.

He cursed, the side of his fist thudding against the wall. How could he get angry with a woman who'd left him with the best of intentions? She loved him. He knew that. Yet here she was, backing out.

Like a slow-motion replay, he ran it in his head for the hundredth time, the issues, the arguments, the tears. But he couldn't get past the woman across from him. He wasted minutes looking at her, memorizing her, just in case.

It was winter outside; she hadn't brought a coat. On a brittle January day, sleet stinging the sidewalks, she'd probably left it at home. She didn't need sweaters or coats. She stood up to him in a thin pin-striped suit and a skin-soft silk blouse.

He remembered all too well how warm-blooded Sara could be. The very idea heated his blood. She'd thrown their bedroom window open year-round, oblivious to the drafts and traffic noises, wearing nothing to bed but her wedding ring, shedding nightgowns and negligees at the merest touch.

Ten years of intimate knowledge of the woman had to give him an advantage. He racked his brain for it. He knew if he confronted her head-on, she'd dig in. He also knew she'd forgiven him in the past, for thoughtlessness, impulsiveness, sheer male thickheadedness. Could she forgive him now? Even if for the life of him he didn't know what he'd done wrong?

They had to start somewhere. He began with his job.

Sportswriting meant constant travel, evenings, weekends, playoffs. It also meant the occasional spin in an Indy race car or a death-defying drop in a hang glider, things she never failed to needle him about when she thought his job took precedence over their marriage.

"Remember when I went skydiving for a story?"

She stopped her pacing and fixed him with a look. "That was a dumb stunt."

"Turned into a great column though." As if that was all that mattered.

She scoffed. "You could have gotten yourself killed."

"Is that why, while I was leaping out of an airplane risking my neck, *you* decided to go shopping?"

"Someone had to pick out your headstone."

"You always could bring me down to earth."

"So could gravity."

He barked a laugh. He loved it when she acted sassy. Nine times out of ten, he had it coming.

"New place at the mall," she added. "Monuments 'R' Us. They were having a sale."

"I couldn't have done it without you," he said sincerely.

She combed an unruly curl off her forehead by way of accepting his compliment. "And here I thought you were about to apologize for putting me through hell six years ago. I had nightmares for months."

"Some of my best memories are of soothing them late at night."

She met his softly spoken comment with a glower. "That wasn't intended as a reward."

"No?" He unbuttoned his sport coat, the better to sling it back and slide his hands into his pockets.

Her gaze skimmed him quickly. Her cheeks colored when he caught her. She gave her reflection a quelling glare. "You'd risk your fool neck for ten inches of print."

"I love my column."

"Don't I know it."

He considered spouting off about sports and getting paid for doing what he loved, the best job in the world. He was good at it. But the day the skydiving column appeared, he'd found himself walking around all afternoon with a bad case of butterflies, wondering what Sara would think, if she'd understand what that jump really had meant to him. He told her again, as if for the first time.

"The plane doors opened. The air hit me. I jumped, this bottomless-pit sensation in my stomach. The ground rushed at me. The chute opened. Jerked tight. 'When I finally hit the ground and stood up, my knees shook so hard, I felt like crouching down and kissing the grass. Or finding my wife and kissing her.'" He watched her eyes as he quoted the last two lines. "I wanted the whole world to know how much I loved you."

Her cheeks reddened as she tapped the rail. "People at the office teased me for days. Even Judge Rickers mentioned it. In court."

"I loved you. That's what jumping out of a plane at ten thousand feet taught me."

She spared him a glance in the mirror. "I thought it was 'The bigger they are, the harder they fall'?"

"Make fun," he retorted, recognizing her tactics. The closer they got to emotional truths, the snappier her comebacks became. "I meant all of it," he added.

"And a sports column was the place to tell me."

"What about here?" He watched her eyes, silently dreading the phrase "It's too late." He cut her off before she could say it. "Remember what it felt like falling in this elevator? That's what it felt like falling from a plane. Scary as hell, wondering if the safety mechanisms would work. All I wanted, then and today, was to be with you. I'm glad I was, Sara."

Her heart squeezed tight in her chest. She rested her forehead against the soothing coolness of the mirror. Past tense, she thought. *I'm glad I was.* Was that why he wanted to talk? To sum it up so they could lay it to rest, put their marriage behind them once and for all? For a moment she'd thought he wanted to face the issues that drove them apart. Damn her heart for getting her hopes up because of one kiss.

"So you wanted to take me down with you," she said.

He slowly shook his head, holding her gaze in the mirror. Glib retorts couldn't put distance between them. "You *were* with me. Every time. Running from the bulls in Pamplona, riding a sled in the Iditarod, yacht racing off Florida in a gale-force storm, you were there, Sara. In my heart."

Past tense, she repeated silently, fighting the tug of intimacy in his eyes. His job had taken him halfway across the country. Apparently he needed to sum this up before moving on emotionally. "You expected me to wait patiently at home while you leapt out of airplanes."

"My editor loved the idea. I couldn't back out."

"Did I ever ask you to?"

"No."

As if controlling her hair controlled her unruly emotions, she poked a rebellious strand among a tangle of curls. "Your skydiving expedition did not ruin our marriage."

"Not even when I teased you about doing it again?"

"You think I took that seriously? You don't like heights. I know this. I've seen you turn green when your mother asks you to bring the Christmas decorations down from the attic."

"So you knew I was kidding?"

"Of course. I may be earnest and plodding and totally unspontaneous, but I do have some sense of humor."

"You do?"

"Don't sound so shocked."

He gazed into the misty distance of the past. "Ah yes. Your one elective in law school, The Uses of Humor 101."

She drummed her precisely manicured fingernails on her suit sleeve. "I must have a sense of humor. I married you, didn't I?"

He laughed out loud, chalking up a point for her.

Sara fought a smile and lost. Bantering with Tony was second nature, familiar as an old bathrobe, comfortable as floppy slippers. She discounted the tartness it added to a conversation, the crackle of temper, the splash of flirtation.

She realized with a shock that she'd never traded barbs with other men. Perhaps she recognized the sexual charge that came with verbal one-upsmanship. Like the tang of orange juice in the morning, it came naturally with Tony.

"You picked the best because you aim high," he said. "That's why you married me. You excel at everything you set your sights on."

Except staying married, she thought dismally. She'd failed that in a hundred ways. The least she could do was make their divorce as painless as possible, even if her stomach roiled like a lava flow and her smile grew as brittle as cooling glass.

Face it, he wanted a nostalgic postmortem, not a reconciliation. "I can't tell you what went wrong," she murmured. "By the end, everything seemed wrong."

Tony's hopes sank as her shoulders slumped. He'd thought tackling the little issues first would make it easier. It hadn't. She didn't get it. Maybe she didn't want to. Maybe he was being purposely dense and stubborn, the two qualities she'd accused him of more than once.

He refused to give in. A sixth sense he never mistrusted told him she still cared. After all, she'd thrown herself in his arms when the elevator fell. Did he need a referee throwing his arms in the air to signal touchdown?

Yeah, but where else did she have to go? his conscience jeered.

She'd responded to his kiss, he argued silently.

Until she'd decided the far corner was a safer place to be. She'd kept securely to her side of the elevator ever since. Five feet away and he couldn't reach her. He streaked a hand through his hair, totally lost.

"Our marriage," she stated, grudgingly tossing him a lifeline. "You wanted to talk about why it didn't work."

On the contrary. He wanted to get down on his knees and convince her it still could. "You distracted me."

"It isn't hard distracting someone with the attention span of a mayfly."

"Hey." He employed his best injured tone, all the while drinking in her saucy stance. She'd decided to duel with him, to keep it light and impersonal, make it easy on them both.

It hurt like hell. There'd been a time when a simple encounter wouldn't have involved all this analysis, constantly second-guessing her motives and meanings. There'd been a time when "I love you" meant just that.

"Mayfly remark hit too close to home?" she asked blithely.

Let her be the one with plans and strategies; he'd trust his gut instinct. "Too suggestive," he countered. "Mayflies meet, mate, and die in one day. If I was a fly, I wouldn't be wasting my time with talk."

His hot-blooded Sara flushed like a lit match. "You aren't suggesting—" She shook her head, dislodging the very idea. "I swear, you could flirt during a hurricane."

"Did I ever mention the blonde who sailed with us off the coast of Florida?"

"Every time you want to make me jealous. She was gorgeous and vivacious and tall—"

"And willowy, and statuesque—"

"Thank you, Mr. Thesaurus. She was everything the swimsuit issue searches for, and you never laid a hand on her."

"Just that tiny boost when she climbed the rigging."

"Very funny. You're as faithful and steady as *The New York Times* and you know it."

"Then you know I love you. I never stopped."

She knew. He saw it in her eyes. So what? The clock still ran, all time-outs called. Sara was the organizer, analyzing, categorizing, weighing the pros and cons. The previous year she'd put herself in one column and him in the other. And subtracted.

Him? He was running on pure emotion. A St. Jude medal burned a hole in his pocket. He was grasping at straws, trying to save two lives. "We'll flip a coin. Heads we stay. Tails we wait."

She laughed at the options. "We've talked before, Tony."

"And argued."

"And argued some more."

The And Game. He picked up on it faster than a fumbled football. She'd gotten it out of a marriage manual two weeks before their wedding, then studiously employed it each month thereafter as a means of enhancing communication. The idea was to meet each statement with the word "and," probing for deeper meanings. *His* idea had been to move her analytical sessions to a bubble-filled bathtub and take it from there.

"So we argued," he stated, keeping the conversation afloat. "And?"

"We bickered."

"And blamed each other."

"And got further and further apart instead of closer together. Talking doesn't work, Tony. I rest my case."

He wouldn't let her off that easy, no matter how tiredly she whispered the words. "And, Sara?"

"And you rested yours when you walked out."

His teeth clenched, cutting off a curse. "Okay, so I didn't handle it right. How do you handle a marriage that's falling apart?"

She kicked her briefcase with the toe of her pointed shoe. "If I knew—"

"Not with lawyers," he said.

"And not with blame."

"So we start again. Heads, we talk about it. Tails, we discuss it."

She huffed and snatched the offered coin from his fingers. She flipped it so high, it pinged off the metal slats that held the acoustic tiles to the ceiling. Tony caught it. Sara didn't move. Her head remained tilted back, her mouth open in surprise. "Hey! There's a door up there."

Tony craned his neck. All he saw were twelve equal squares dotted with pinprick-sized holes and surrounded by a thin slat of walnut trim.

"There's always an access door in the ceiling of an elevator," Sara said.

"In the movies, maybe."

"We could look."

And she could escape him even quicker. "Why don't we wait until the experts fix it."

"Haven't you heard of resourcefulness? Let's see what *we* can do."

He seized the word "we" and held on. Wasn't teamwork the best way to forge lifelong bonds? Working together might bring them closer together. *And the Cubs might win the next World Series.* Long shots were the only shots he had left. And if she found a way out?

"We'll pull down three tiles," he stated. "I'm not dismantling this whole thing."

She agreed.

Tony stripped off his coat, tossing it in the corner. His tie landed after it, the pink-and-black floral print clashing with the sedate burgundy lining.

Needless to say, she'd picked out the coat, he the eye-catching tie. He rebelled against the noose-wearing custom by flaunting the ugliest ties he could find, his travels regularly uncovering hideous new alternatives.

Sara remembered. The flash of pink, white, and black against his cotton shirt reminded her how pale and gray the corner of the closet had become when he'd taken his slashes of color and moved out.

She watched him roll up his sleeves before resolutely focusing on the ceiling. "We'll take one tile from each row," she announced. "That one, that one, and, uh, that one."

"You always did make up your mind fast."

Not when it came to the divorce. And not, she noticed, when it came to discussing their failed marriage. Although she'd anguished over it for a year, she was curiously reticent to dissect it here. Memories were all she had left. She didn't want them tarnished.

But memories were only life's dreams. They dissipated quickly when faced with reality. A slew of ugly ties in the closet, a splash of bay rum aftershave wafting through the bathroom, what were they compared to Tony standing two feet away? Love had a way of skewing a person's perceptions. She wouldn't know if he really wanted her back until they stood in Melchior's office, their divorce decree waiting to be signed. Maybe that explained her hurry to see what lay beyond those ceiling tiles.

Stretching as tall as her stilettos allowed, Sara pushed one up with her briefcase, cursing under her breath. "I can't reach it."

Tony rested his hands on his lean hips. "Set your fanny on my shoulder."

"What?" She brought the briefcase between them like a gladiator's shield.

"I can't reach it myself, and you definitely can't reach it, short stuff. Hop up here. I'll raise you so you can play with your tiles."

"Paretti, you've got a great set of shoulders, but there's no way my hip size will balance on just one of them."

"Then sit on both. Wrap your legs around my neck."

The color drained from her cheeks.

"Okay, okay. Stand on my knee." He got down on one knee, the other forming a stair step for Sara. "But first take off the stilettos. I'm not getting gored."

She shot a frustrated glance at the ceiling and a dubious one at his knee. With a decisive huff, she set the briefcase in her own corner and stripped off her suit coat. She'd be resourceful, methodical, and sensible about this. Until she knew for certain what he wanted, she'd be completely immune to his nearness.

Using one pointed toe to pull down the heel strap of her other shoe, she kicked it off. Then she bent to unsnap the tiny buckle of the remaining shoe, lifting her heel behind her.

Tony sat back as if she'd given him a shove. "Such beautiful feet."

Scowling, she turned aside. "Only you could make ten normal toes on two size-seven feet sound sexy."

"They are. Intimate. Revealing. How many people see your feet naked?"

Her toes dug into the plush carpet for balance. "I have nylons on."

"So I noticed."

Her fingers fumbled with the suddenly tricky buckle. She sensed every inch of her nylons clinging to her legs like Tony's gaze. Charcoal gray might add a severe touch to a pin-striped power suit, but she'd forgotten the unspeakable things it did to Tony in a bedroom.

He rasped the cobwebs out of his throat. "Do you still have that garter belt I bought you?"

She spun around as if bitten. "Honestly."

"Just curious."

"All I'm doing is taking off my shoes. We were married ten years."

"As if that lessens anything."

She couldn't argue with him there. She turned back to the corner, yanking the strap a final time before dropping the other shoe. Maybe it was the year apart. Or maybe it was all the years together. Their attraction pulsed more powerfully than ever, the sultry passionate nights, the lazy afternoons, the stunning mornings suddenly there between them.

Sara thought of a hundred reasons why she was attracted to Tony. She could also talk herself into a world of heartache if she didn't keep her mind on getting out of there. Lust, charm, enjoying the moment—all those things made Tony nearly irresistible. None of them erased the words written on that divorce decree.

She turned, fully cognizant of his languid perusal. All that bending had sent her narrow skirt riding up. She wriggled it back to a respectable length. Ignoring his welcoming smile, she stepped directly toward him, as if the stilettos, the coat, the stern armor were still in place. "Lift me up."

"Always happy to return a favor."

She planted her arch on his thigh. "Dirty old man."

"If I live to be a hundred, you'll still have that effect on me."

"Just do it."

"Here? Now? With pleasure."

"Tony." She withdrew her foot.

He caught her leg, curling his hand around her calf, listening to the hiss of nylon against his warm palm. He placed her foot back on his thigh. "How's this?"

She placed a trembling hand on his shoulder for support, tottering as she reached for the ceiling.

Tony hugged her knees to his chest and hoisted her straight up. "Which tile?"

"To the left. And stop groaning. I only gained five pounds." She bit her lip, wondering if he remembered she ate when she was worried. If he noticed, he kept it to himself.

He stutter-stepped sideways, obeying her terse commands, concentrating on the scraping noises overhead and the pressure of her knees against his chest. She wiggled. He looked up. She raised both hands, canting a tile to direct light into the black outer casing of the elevator. Her breasts rose with the motion. So did his temperature.

She set the tile back. "Next."

He stepped to the right as ordered, waiting patiently while his intrepid explorer searched the new cavity with her customary thoroughness. He could have stood there all day.

He closed his eyes, inhaling slowly, his face inches from her belly. She smelled like her soap and her favorite perfume, honeysuckle and jasmine. He inhaled again, the wool skirt tickling the tip of his nose.

She squirmed, her knee digging in beside one of his nipples. She touched his shoulder briefly, steadying herself with one hand. "Hand me—"

He didn't hear the rest. He didn't care. She said something about needing. He knew need very well. Apparently she'd discovered something. So had he.

"Put me down," she said at last.

"With pleasure." On any bed, any blanket, on satin sheets or deep plush carpet . . .

He slid her back to earth, the backs of her legs straining as she pointed her toes, eager to touch ground. He took advantage of every inch, his arms opening for the flare of her hips, closing on the narrowness of her waist. He abraded his cheek against her wool waistband, then soothed it on the silk folds of her blouse. A lacy bra couldn't disguise her breasts' budded peaks nor the flush of pink where her collar plunged to a V. Her chest rose and fell in fluttery breaths, releasing the fragrance of jasmine and bare skin.

Tony dragged in every sensation, his lungs aching, his body hurting with want. He pressed a kiss to the side of her neck and finished it with a haggard whisper. "Tell me what you want." He needed to touch her, taste her, hold her. But more, he needed to see her eyes when she answered him. He lifted his head.

She held doe-still in his arms. He felt her heart race, saw the apprehension in her eyes, heard it in her half-whispered words. "I want your knife."

FOUR

She was poised to run the moment he eased his grip.
He sensed it. But she made no move; his gentle Sara
wouldn't hurt his feelings by pulling away. A trace of
bitterness coated his tongue. That wasn't the kind of
kindness he wanted. He let her go. "My knife?"

She fastened her gaze on his Adam's apple. "You
still carry your penknife, don't you?"

He rummaged in his pocket and found the compact Swiss Army knife with its red plastic casing. "I'm
flattered you remembered. Plan to carve my heart out
with it?"

"No guilt games. Jewish guilt versus Catholic guilt
is a dead heat, and you know it." She plucked at a thin
metal implement with her manicured nails.

He covered her hand with his. "What are you looking for?"

One glance at his dark brown eyes, and her emotions swelled. She concentrated on the narrow column

of his throat, tracing the rise and fall of a tense swallow. "There's an opening. Up there. I thought we could pry it open."

"I'm all for opening doors."

She shook her head, her nemesis curl bobbing across her forehead, dislodged, uncooperative. Her desire for him had overwhelmed her on too many occasions. She'd wanted it to. Not this time. She'd stick to her plan until she knew for certain he didn't want that divorce. She'd get them into Melchior's office if she had to climb there.

He took the knife from her and found the correct section. "Forget the bottle opener. Try the screwdriver." He rocked back on his heels, peering up into the dead end she'd uncovered, gauging where it might lead. "I suppose you want me to lift you up again."

"If you wouldn't mind."

"Love to."

She brandished the knife as fiercely as a petite Phi Beta Kappa could. "Behave this time."

Crouching, he wrapped his arms around her thighs and lifted her in one move. For an electric moment her face was even with his, her body pressed to every taut muscle he possessed. He poached a kiss, blunt and unapologetic. Then he slid her up his body, inch by tactile inch.

Sara felt the ground fall farther and farther away. Her eyes adjusted to the murky space separating the paneled interior from the industrial outer core. She found the screwdriver and turned the first screw. Her hands trembled as if she were defusing a bomb. Or standing in an elevator with Tony's cheek pressed to her thigh.

She concentrated on the task at hand. At last the

final screw clattered onto the top side of a ceiling tile. She pushed upward with a yip of victory. "I'm through!"

"What's up there?"

"I can't see."

Tony craned his neck. All darkness looked the same. But this darkness smelled different. Dank, musty air from the elevator shaft curled down from the ceiling. The smell of cables and grease added a pungent counterpoint to dust and air too long enclosed. "See any doors above us?"

"Can't say for sure."

"Somebody ought to crawl out there." The minute the words left his mouth, he knew he'd be the one.

So did she. She wriggled around, dropping him a look. "Oh no you don't."

He slid her back down his body. "Sorry, kid. It's in the manual. Macho Men, Volume one. Quote: In dangerous situations, with women in attendance, men stick their necks out like damn fools."

All kidding aside, if Sara really *was* claustrophobic, he'd get them out of there as fast as possible. Her security came first, just like her happiness.

He filched the Swiss Army knife from her delicate fist and dropped it in his shirt pocket. "I'll take a look around."

"Famous last words. I think we should think about this."

"Time for action." An Italian Superman about to leap tall buildings, he jumped straight up. His hands caught then slid off the metal edge. He hissed a curse.

"Careful!" Sara grasped his hand between hers, peering at the scrape.

"It's nothing."

"It's cut. You could have metal slivers in there. When was the last time you had a tetanus shot?"

"About the same time you fussed over me this way."

She scowled, peering at the angry red scrape, a palm-reading Florence Nightingale.

"What was that word you invented for someone who obsesses about other people's health?" Tony asked.

"Philo-hypochondriac."

"I believe the layman's term is 'Jewish mother.' "

Caught caring, she dropped his hand. "You'll live."

"And I love you, too, Princess." He didn't wait for her reaction. The coward in him decided climbing on suspended roofs was safer than sticking around in the elevator. He slapped his hands together, ignoring the temporary sting. "A forty-inch vertical leap should get me there. Michael Jordan does it all the time."

"That's why he gets paid millions and you get paid tens."

"When a horse throws you, you get right back on."

"When an elevator throws you, you fall thirty-nine floors. I don't think this is such a good idea."

He lifted her chin with a touch. "Sara, I'm going out there. It may not be pretty. I may not come back. If anything happens, I wanted you to know—"

She rolled those big brown eyes. "Enough already. Get out there."

He chuckled and showed her what he needed. "Link your fingers like this and give me a boost."

When she'd done as asked, he gripped the outer

skin of the metal shell and lifted himself through the hatch. Bracing himself with his elbows, he looked left to right in the sudden blackness. The smells were stronger there, the sense of emptiness immense, nearly palpable. Suffocating darkness hovered over him like a velvet curtain. The cloth tore, a blinding slit. "Whoa."

Sidestepping his dangling feet, Sara instantly picked up the excitement in his voice. "What is it?"

"Light. An elevator door opened about ten floors up." He grunted and his feet lifted out of sight.

Sara listened to him shuffle across the ceiling on what she hoped were his hands and knees. "Tony?"

"This whole shaft is one black corridor, like a mail chute running up the inside of the building. I can't see the side walls, but there were six elevators in the hall downstairs. They must slide by us on both sides. Here comes one now. It's like a glowing box lowered on strings."

Sara sighed and stared at the ceiling. "I knew I married a writer for a reason. Is there anything less poetic up there? Like access doors?"

"Ooh."

He sounded like a one-man audience at a fireworks display. Sara danced back and forth on tiptoe. "Ooh what?"

"The lights."

"Tony!" A thud and a grunt almost stopped Sara's heart. "Tony?"

"Worried?" His face popped into the black square above her, a goofy grin on his face.

She glared. "I just don't want to be trapped in here alone if you do something dumb."

"Like swing from cable to cable doing my Tarzan

imitation? Don't worry. Look, here comes another one. Let's see where it stops."

"You go ahead; I can't see a thing." She paced a rut in the spot directly below the opening. "I'll stay here and wait for the play-by-play."

She'd done that on plenty of nights. He'd come home from a road trip or a game, buzzing from the excitement of competition, delighting in telling her about it. She caught on quick; she was his sounding board. If she yawned, that section of the story never showed up in his column.

Sara had always prized herself on being self-sufficient, cuddling up with a briefcase of work or a treasured novel whenever he was out of town. But there was no denying how a ringing telephone had buoyed her, his quick check-in from the road elevating her entire evening.

She hadn't minded being his unacknowledged editor. When he told her about the games and the personalities involved, he also listened. He valued her judgment and she valued his. She'd always trusted him when he was away. Always stayed busy until he came home. And always, always missed him like the devil.

"That damn job," she muttered. "He's probably taking notes up there."

She couldn't curse his column too much. When their attempts to resolve their problems had ended in tears and slamming doors and the terrible oppressive silence that followed, she'd clung to his words, poring over his articles as if features on baseball arbitration were love letters, endlessly unfolded and reread, memorized, wept over.

The ceiling creaked. He sucked in a breath. She held hers. Craning her neck, she saw a swath of light cut through the darkness directly above them. Doors opened where no elevator had stopped. Three stories up, she made out the shapes of four men in the wide glow of a doorway.

"Hello!" they called.

"Mistuh Paretti. You hear us, mon?"

"Roberto!" Sara's heart clogged in her throat. She'd become inexplicably but undeniably attached to that Jamaican accent.

"Right here," Tony called.

The sound of that rich baritone affected her even more.

A flashlight shone down, silhouetting Tony's face as he crouched near the hatch. Sara saw his arm go up, shielding him from the blazing light.

"What are you doing outside the elevator?" a low voice demanded.

"Looking for a way out," Tony responded.

"Please get inside the car this instant. The liability should you fall—"

Sara frowned. The boom of the third male voice sounded oddly familiar. However, her attention instantly transferred to Tony as he squirmed back inside. He dropped to a crouch, then straightened to his full six feet one inch.

She hadn't seriously thought he was in danger, not for a minute. It was inexcusable the way her arms wound around his neck, her cheek pressing his until his faint afternoon stubble rasped roughly against her skin. "Just one big light show, huh?"

"No problem," he lied.

She felt the sickly coolness of his cheek, the faint sheen of perspiration. Her throat grew tight, her grip tighter. "My hero."

His bear hug nearly knocked the wind out of her. For a second she thought he'd say something. But he seemed to think better of it, temporarily more concerned with their audience above. Draping one arm heavily around her shoulder, he placed his other hand on his hip and shouted to their rescuers. "You took so long, we decided to help ourselves."

"Please don't do that again. There are experts who can solve this much more efficiently than you."

Sara gulped. That pompous dictatorial tone disguised as stuffy concern was none other than Michael Melchior, her attorney. She'd told Roberto they had an appointment with him, not to go get him.

"So where are your so-called experts?" Tony demanded.

"Right here," Melchior said.

Sara caught sight of four husky silhouettes stepping back to confer. She picked out Roberto and DuWayne by their overalls. Michael Melchior was the short balding one in the black funeral suit. A gold watch chain flickered across his ample abdomen. He was forty-five, dressed sixty-five, and had been asking her out for two months now. Darned if she could remember a single restaurant they'd eaten at or a show they'd seen. Not with Tony beside her, his body sinewy and lean inside his clothes, his scent sweeter than a drug.

They'd never even kissed. Still tasting Tony's lips on hers, she couldn't imagine they ever would. There was only one man who'd ever made her feel so sensuous, so earthy, who took her to another world with one breath-stealing caress.

"Who's that?" Tony murmured, his voice so near her ear that she shuddered.

She glanced at the fourth figure conferring with Michael, then tilted her head to answer Tony. Her lips almost skimmed his. "The engineer, I think."

"Ah." He looked up.

Sara immediately wanted the hatch closed, their cocoon unbroken. That couldn't be the engineer. They couldn't be rescued yet. There was so much to say. She stood beside Tony, drinking him in, comparing the pale fantasies she'd lived on for the last twelve months to the real man. She wanted to hold on to someone who'd made her happier than she'd ever been. Was that so wrong?

But the men above had jobs to do. Obviously they thought fixing a recalcitrant piece of hardware took precedence over repairing a ten-year love affair, over mending resentments, cementing a commitment that had crumbled. *Save that*, she thought wildly. *Repair this*.

The conferring group returned to the doorway ledge. Tony squeezed her shoulder. She squinted up, blinking rapidly.

"This is Richard Scott," Melchior announced.

A young man with carrot-red hair waved at them. A windbreaker dangled from one hand, revealing his white short-sleeved shirt and pocket protector. From this severe angle Sara knew she couldn't detect white socks beneath his brown pants. Nevertheless, the man was a walking stereotype of the studious engineer. He looked as if he'd bicycled there. She tried to feel reassured.

"What's the prognosis, doc?" Tony shouted.

The young man shoved his glasses up his nose with his thumb. "We've been going over the options that would get you out of there quickest. However, due to the sultan's private floors, we're presented with some challenges."

"Sultan?"

"The Sultan of Surama maintains three private floors in this building. For security reasons, only one elevator stops at those floors. The rest of the doors have been closed off."

"Then open them."

" 'Walled off' might be a better term. We'd have to break through brick. You're better off being lifted or waiting until we get the cable mechanism working again."

"What's lifted?"

"We attach a winch to this wall and haul you from your car up to this floor in harnesses."

"No, thank you," Sara replied.

"They're the kind the fire department uses," Scott said encouragingly.

Sara watched the freckled young man thumb his glasses up his nose again. Was he sweating? She shivered. "I know your heart is in the right place"—right behind his pocket protector and its slew of ballpoint pens and mechanical pencils, she thought—"but I don't relish the idea of swinging out over this abyss in some contraption made of leather straps."

"Nylon. It's perfectly safe. Not that anything's perfect, but—"

"Are we safe here?" Tony interrupted. "Is this thing going to drop?"

"No way. The brakes are totally sound." A flashlight played across the cables, its beam making Sara and Tony flinch as it swept across their faces.

"I'll take your word for it," Tony replied. He wasn't in any hurry to get out just yet. Sara was talking to him, teasing him, letting him hold her as if their being a couple were the most natural thing in the world. The people up there saw that. If he and Sara could stand by each other a while longer, she'd see it too. All she had to do was look in the mirror.

But Sara, being Sara, exhausted every angle first. "What are our other options?"

"Well, this is a little trickier," Scott said. "We can stop a car beside yours, have someone climb out the top, as you two managed, then shove planks across. You'd climb over from your disabled car to a working one and be out of there in, oh, twenty minutes."

"You'd be having coffee in our offices in less than half an hour," Melchior added.

"Whoa, back up," Tony said. "Planks?"

Sara bobbed her head in time with his. "Planks?"

"Two at least," the young man insisted. "Twelve inches each. You'd crawl across. In harness, of course, just in case—"

"Just in case," Sara muttered.

"How far is it between cars?" Tony asked.

"Six feet. We don't build them too close together or they'd scrape as they passed."

Tony studied the floor as he paced off the distance between the doors and the back wall. His gaze leveled on Sara. "This is five feet. Think you could do it?"

She stared at the carpet as if a gaping black abyss opened on all sides with two narrow planks spanning it. "Could you?"

"I'd be behind you all the way."

She didn't doubt it, not when she saw the commitment in his eyes.

"You were the gymnast," he reminded her.

"In high school."

"You did cartwheels across a balance beam."

"And you climbed the ten-meter diving platform at the Barcelona Olympics, froze, and had to be talked down by Greg Louganis. Another stunt for your column."

He grimaced. "It didn't look that high on TV."

"I'm amazed you crawled out there in the first place." She tilted her chin at the ceiling.

He shrugged, as if death-defying deeds were daily fare. "You needed me to."

Touched, she wrestled with the tender feelings his offhand courage evoked. "I never asked."

He skimmed her cheek with the backs of his fingers. "Some things you don't need to ask."

Her eyes grew round, unspoken hurts lurking in their depths. "And some things you shouldn't have to." Like *Do you love me?* And *Do you really want this divorce?* That question in particular shouted in her mind. She stepped out of his arms, clamping her lips shut to avoid making yet another fool of herself where Tony was concerned. It was over.

Just not yet. They were trapped here until Michael and his engineer came up with a better solution. Sara stepped firmly into the center of the car. "We'll wait here," she called.

Tony touched her arm. "If they can get you down, go."

"You won't get rid of me that easily."

"I'm not the one who's claustrophobic."

"That's because you have someone else's fear to focus on. You always think of other people first. What happens when I leave and you've got nothing to think about but the walls closing in?"

"You mean like when we split up and I got my own apartment?"

She wouldn't hide from the pain in his eyes, not when she'd put it there. "Tony—"

"Divorce or no divorce, I want you to be safe."

"And I don't want to be out there worrying about you trapped in here. We go together or we don't go at all."

"You'll stay with me?"

Yes, she wanted to shout. She wanted to stay with him, to fold up in his arms and never leave. "We stay until this is fixed."

He tucked her in the crook of his arm. "Looks as if we're in this together. Till death or technology do us part."

"May I remind you," Melchior rumbled, "that Mr. Scott has offered a viable method of escape? Sara, my dear, as your lawyer I must advise you—"

Tony let her go so fast, Sara had to catch herself by digging her bare heels in the plush carpet. "Your lawyer!" he howled.

"I told Roberto we had an appointment," she explained hastily. "I didn't expect him to go fetch him."

Tony shoved a hand through his already disheveled hair, one black lock falling on his forehead like an exclamation point. "Your lawyer's negotiating our release. Or *your* release."

"That isn't fair."

"Isn't it?" Heaving a sigh, he raked a gaze around their enclosed space. "I guess this won't be the first time your lawyers have screwed me."

Quick to defend the unfairly accused, Sara jumped to Melchior's defense. "His office has been very decent to us, and you know it. They aren't charging me a fraction of what they could have. They haven't harassed you about alimony or support—"

"Unlike Mr. Paretti," Melchior interrupted, "who has taken numerous opportunities to harass *us*."

"You what?" Sara turned on him.

Tony spun on his heel, evading her outraged glare. "That's it, Melchior. Trap me like a rat, then gloat over me."

"He is not here to taunt you," she insisted. "I'm sure he's only here because his firm owns the building and he knows me."

"Owns it?!"

Uh-oh, she thought. Faster than she could say "volatile," Tony's anger transformed itself into sheer glee. His rattling laugh made her blood run cold. "Tony, what are you thinking?"

Hands splayed on his waist, he took up position directly in sight of Melchior. "You're in for it now, bud!"

"Are you addressing me, sir?"

"Yeah, you! You raised-letter-stationery-sending, padded-billing, plush-penthouse-officed ambulance-chaser you. You're in trouble now."

"Uh, Tony—"

"You draw up my wife's divorce, then trap me in an elevator in *your* building. I claim conflict of interest. Wrongful imprisonment. I claim pain and suffering. Negligence! I'll sue the pants off the elevator company, the engineers, and every last man who owns this place."

Sara gave his sleeve a yank. "I'm sure they're limited partners."

The fine legal distinction barely slowed him down.

"Unlike the damages I'm claiming, which are *un*limited, you bloodsucking bastards."

"Tony!"

"Hush, sweetheart, I'm on a roll."

"Mr. Paretti," Melchior put in. "You have been advised of two methods of egress, which you have declined to pursue. I have witnesses who will attest to that. As for Ms. Cohen, I advise her in the strongest terms to move to other quarters. As your lawyer, Sara, I believe it's in your best interest to be as far as possible from this man."

Tony couldn't have yelped louder if an elephant had stomped on his toe. "What?"

"We've had dealings with him before at Melchior, Kravitz, and Keene. Unpleasant dealings. He's accosted members of my firm via the U.S. mails and made abusive and threatening phone calls—"

Aghast, Sara turned on Tony. "When did this happen?"

"Last year," he muttered. He ran a hand over his mouth as if the memory left a bitter taste. "After we separated. I didn't know you'd planned on filing for divorce so soon."

"But you'd moved to Chicago. I thought it was over."

"Did I have to get a certified letter *telling* me that? You could have warned me it was coming."

"I didn't have your number."

"*They* did."

She swung back to the hatchway. "Michael! Why didn't you tell me?"

"I didn't wish to disturb you, my dear. Men undergoing the strain of divorce can be highly unstable. It is always best to let your lawyer handle all contacts on your behalf as an objective intermediary."

Sara and Tony stared at each other a long moment.

"You would have called me?" he asked, those awful months suddenly cast in a new light.

"You were upset?" she asked.

"He was dangerous." Melchior's rumbling voice blundered into their confusion. "Considering his history with my firm, Sara, my dear, you might be a good deal safer crawling across a board thirty-nine stories up than remaining with someone of such a volatile nature."

"I would never hurt my wife," Tony bellowed.

"He would never hurt me," Sara agreed, blushing nevertheless at the stream of profanity, Italian and English, erupting from Tony's mouth at the very suggestion he'd lay a hand on Sara.

"See this, Melchior?" Tony planted his feet directly beneath the opening and swung his forearm up, catching his biceps in an unmistakable gesture known to cab drivers around the world.

"See?" Michael sniffed. "Violent already."

Outrage overcoming her common sense, Sara literally shoved Tony aside. "Michael Melchior, I have never claimed Tony was violent. You're stirring up trouble that didn't even exist until you poked your nose into it!"

"Typical lawyer," Tony muttered.

"And you're no better than he is," she snapped.

"Maybe I should get my own lawyer," Tony announced. "Sue Melchior, Kravitz, *and* Keene."

"You don't even have a lawyer," Sara replied tartly.

"I know plenty."

"Sports attorneys and agents," she scoffed. "They don't even pick up the phone for less than a million dollars."

"My kinda guys. Heck, I could even hire you. You're the expert. Hey, Melchior, I'd like you to meet my wife. She defends tenants against negligent landlords every day of the week."

Sara stiffened as Tony put an arm around her shoulders. Did he say "my wife"?

"Hold on a minute," the young engineer piped up. "We repaired this unit just last month—"

"So you *knew* it wasn't working. Where were the signs saying Board at Your Own Risk? I call that negligence, slipshod management."

Sara squirmed, the words "my wife" echoing in her heart. Did he still consider her his wife? He'd accepted their separation so coolly. No one had told her about his outbursts at the law offices. She understood their trying to shield her. What she'd never understood was Tony's silence regarding the divorce. It was so unlike him.

She studied him as his diatribe against Melchior died down. This was more like the Tony she knew, every emotion on the surface.

But there were other matters to settle at present. A yawning silence had descended, and she seemed to be at the center of it. She directed a pained smile toward the ceiling. "Technically, he might have a case, Michael."

A "humph" sounded above them. "It was repaired in good faith not four weeks ago. Besides, you've been presented with every opportunity to exit it. If the two of you choose to remain longer, it's out of my hands."

Sara's spine grew rigid. "Don't you bully us, Michael. You're responsible for the upkeep of this building and the safety of its inhabitants. If we choose not to exercise the plank option, that in no way absolves you of liability nor the responsibility to seek further solutions."

Tony grinned from ear to ear, bending down to nibble hers. "God, you're good at this."

She brushed him off with an impatient wave of her hand. "Mr. Scott? What else do you have in mind? Options, please."

"Uh, we'll have to go to the top floor. That's where the main housings are for the controls. We can't release the brake until we know for sure we can move the elevator to another floor."

"Is that it?"

"It might take some time."

"Then please proceed. We'll wait here."

"Yes, ma'am."

"Good day, Michael."

Melchior grumbled something and stepped back from the ledge. The doors hushed closed. Staring at the darkness above them, Sara strode to her corner. Arms crossed, eyes closed, she rested her back against the corner rail.

After the acrimonious exchange, silence settled around her and Tony like a down comforter.

He watched her pinch the bridge of her nose with her thumb and forefinger. "You look the way you used to when you came home from a tough day in court."

Eyes closed, she wagged her head back and forth. "I never thought I'd be building a case against my own attorneys."

"It's their building, their responsibility."

"Did you have to resort to that hand gesture?"

"Bet that doesn't happen to him every day of the week."

Their laughter filled the elevator, then died softly. "Neither does this," she whispered, watching him, breath bated, waiting for him to make any kind of move, to repeat the words he'd said a moment ago without thinking. *My wife.*

He came closer. Two steps brought him directly before her. He drew a finger down her cheek. "Sorry I lost my temper, but when he suggested I'd hurt you—"

She broke eye contact, seeking the endlessly repeated walls reflected in the mirrors. "You'd never hurt me. Not that way."

But he had some other way. Tony knew that as well as he knew the lineup of this season's Yankees. When had it started? When had he given up on them, slinking off to Chicago and pretending to start over? When the papers had arrived, he'd never had the courage to simply call her and ask why, too afraid of the answer he might get. As long as she didn't come right out and say "I don't love you anymore," he could pretend ten years of his life hadn't been squandered.

Her voice brought him back to the present. "Michael was way out of line. You may have a temper, you may get a little volatile sometimes—"

"Only on days ending in *y.*"

"Storms blow over fast with you."

"Then why—?" What had driven them so far apart? The question hung over them as surely as the elevator dangled in midair. He drew her into his arms. "Whatever happens, we're in this together. I mean that."

He felt her gather herself, one last barrier to protect her from him. "You mean until you sign the papers?"

"I won't sign."

She clutched the sides of his shirt in her hands. "Damn you, Tony, don't do this to me."

"Do what?"

Her eyes blurred with tears. "Don't pretend you love me."

FIVE

She broke away, pushing out from between him and the cold reflective walls. It hurt too much. She wanted it too much. Letting him go had been the hardest thing she'd ever done. She'd never be able to do it twice.

"I never stopped loving you," he said.

She was the one who had to stop, to think things out, weighing for the hundredth time whether she could risk loving him again. "You left," she said, catching his nod in the mirror.

"It seemed like the only thing to do. God knows I couldn't do anything else right."

Tension crept into the elevator, slithering in on the rasp of his voice, the outline of his fists shoved into his pockets, the familiar sound of blame. Maybe it was time they faced what really happened.

Sara faced Tony. Her hands curved around the rail behind her, fingernails scraping the hollow brass. "It wasn't pretty, was it? Our breaking up."

"A grand-prize, all-expenses-paid vacation in Hell."
"You packed up and left."
"You asked me to."

They'd been up all night arguing, him yelling, her crying. A drizzly January dawn cast an oppressive gray light over their bedroom. They made feverish love before dawn, both sensing it was for the last time. He didn't even finish. Like his refusal to talk, she took that as another form of withdrawal.

She spoke first. "It seems like everything we say, or don't say, we end up hurting each other more."

"What do you want me to do about it?" he snapped.

She flinched as if he'd slapped her. "We have to stop doing this. You won't talk about—"

"What does it help?" He sat on the edge of the bed, staring at his open suitcase. He had a road trip, two weeks in Miami covering the Super Bowl. Damn him if he wasn't looking forward to it, a chance to get away, to breathe again.

She sat up, holding the sheet to her breasts, staring at the suitcase as if he were leaving her for good. A sense of failure hung over the room, stale as cigarette smoke. Neither knew whether to lash out or hold on tighter. Like drowning lovers, they dragged each other down.

Sara spoke into the silence. "When you come back, I want you to think about getting another apartment."

He took it like a punch to the stomach, turning away before she saw how much it hurt. "Sure. Why not?" His back to her, he slapped underwear into his case, socks, T-shirts, anything he could get his hands on. The dull thud of cotton absorbed the roughness in his voice. "You know, I've been offered a job in Chicago. Again."

If he heard her gasp, it didn't register. He plucked a handful of ties from the rack in the closet. The Sun-Times wanted him even if she didn't. "Maybe I'll take them up on it. Find an apartment there. How would you like that?"

She stifled a cry, rushing past him into the bathroom, slamming the door. She turned on the faucet full blast, the roaring water drowning her sobs. She kept hoping he'd hear, that he'd knock quietly and say "Sara, let me in."

Instead he calmly finished dressing. The suitcase clicked shut, followed by the apartment door.

In the elevator, Tony remembered it differently. "You wanted me to go."

She blinked, her mouth opened on a tiny gasp of surprise. "I asked if you wanted a separation, that was all."

"Same thing."

"We'd been arguing for months. Time apart seemed to be the best solution."

"So you hit first. The best defense is a good offense, right?"

"I asked you to think about it. You're the one who was so eager to take me up on it. You got on the first elevator that came along."

Oh yeah? Tony thought. He'd waited for three of them, pressing the button, waving them away. Finally the elevator man told him to get on or go home. He didn't have a home anymore. He got on. "How would you know which elevator I took?"

She averted her gaze, folding her arms more securely, holding down a shrug. "By the time I got down the hall, you were gone."

She'd come running after him. He hadn't known that. "I know you when your mind's made up, *cara*. There didn't seem to be any point in arguing about that too."

"You seemed so eager to start over someplace else."

"I couldn't take New York without you. Do you have any idea what it's like to look into a million faces, hoping to see just one?"

Her eyes told him she did. She had.

He almost stepped toward her. His feet wouldn't move.

"You never called," she said.

"I was waiting for your call."

"You didn't give me your new number."

"Ma said she gave it to you."

"But *you* didn't. If you'd wanted me to call, you would've told it to me yourself."

"That would've meant calling first." He laughed, a harsh sound that let neither one of them off the hook. "Chalk up another one to stubborn pride."

"Were we both wrong?"

"Only in about one hundred different ways." He turned back to the wall. His next words landed like stones on cement, cold and unyielding. "You filed for the divorce fast enough."

"I thought it was what you wanted. You left—"

"—because walking out was easier than staying. We went over the same ground time and again."

"Yes." Sara rubbed her forehead, picturing the ground that divided them, a ravine as deep and wide as a child-sized grave. "The baby."

"The miscarriage," he corrected her.

She threw her hands up. "We can't even agree on what to call it."

"That didn't stop us from talking about it constantly. You wouldn't get over losing it."

"Don't you dare blame me for grieving."

"You blamed me for not grieving enough."

They both stopped short, their voices echoing sharp over their heads, brittle as icicles. Sara gripped the rail behind her, the tears backing up in her throat.

"So this is my fault," Tony concluded, that too-familiar look of accusation and suffering clouding his eyes.

"I never said that."

"You filed."

"You wouldn't talk to me. Not before. Not after. When I lost the baby, I needed you—"

He turned away, cutting off their discussion. Whether from pain or anger, she couldn't tell. She knew it hurt him to talk about it, that just listening to her weep cut through him like a knife. Why did she insist on talking about it when she knew it hurt him? Because it hurt too much to keep it in. Why couldn't he understand that? "I carried that baby for six months, Tony. It was mine."

"Not ours?"

She let the back of her head thump softly against the mirror, squeezing her eyes shut in frustration. "I'm sorry. I meant ours."

"Right."

She stared at him, silently pleading. There had to be a way to get through one discussion about the baby without it descending into blame and anguish. "We're doing it again."

He shrugged, a pained smile on his face. "We should be experts by now."

"Where did we go wrong?"

"The doctor said—"

"I don't mean the baby. I mean talking about it. Why can't we just talk?"

His shoulders tensed, the lines in his face etched in shadows and creases. "We talked."

"We argued and we blamed each other."

"You cried."

"And you avoided it. We never *dealt* with it."

"Ha." He shoved off from the wall, pacing the side farthest from her, keeping his gaze on the deep blue carpet, his footprints denting it, then disappearing into it. "We did nothing *but* deal with it. For six months it's all we ever talked about. The baby this, the baby that. We talked it to death."

She winced.

He instantly berated himself. "Sorry."

The old pain gnawed at the edges of a composure she was determined to maintain. This was it, her heart insisted, the core of their sorrow. If they didn't face it now, they risked losing their marriage. "A marriage thrives on communication. People who can't talk to each other can't—"

"*Cara*." He practically begged. "Don't start again. Please. We tried. Isn't that enough?"

"No," she insisted. "Not if it ends this way."

"All you ever wanted to talk about was the baby. Not us. We can't bring it back, and it's killing everything else we had."

She knew the words; he'd said them before. He'd listened to her weep until he couldn't listen anymore. After six months he'd suggested she "get over it."

So had her doctor, her parents, her friends. People seemed to think a miscarriage wasn't a baby, it wasn't real until it had a birthday and a hospital bracelet. It had been to her.

But not to Tony, she thought, a pang dividing her heart. They were so different, approaching life from such different angles. She analyzed it; he lived it. After the miscarriage he'd tried making her laugh, or forget. Never, she'd argued, throwing the well-intentioned words in his face. How could he even suggest they forget something so precious?

He suggested they have another. The very idea stopped her cold. What if she lost that one? And what if Tony reacted by wrapping his feelings in the same distance and unconcern? She couldn't do it alone, not again.

But she'd be just as alone if they went through with the divorce. Sara struggled to see things from a new angle. "Maybe it was my fault, obsessing over something I'd lost."

"The baby meant a lot to you," he said, fumbling, too, reaching for the right thing to say. "There comes a time—"

"Rabbi Kushman said there was no set way to mourn, no time period—"

"Sooner or later you've got to move on."

"And move away?"

Tony sighed. His hands hung uselessly at his sides. There had to be a way. "Our marriage is like this damn elevator. We're trapped in it together, but damned if I can think of a way out."

"Try."

"Do you want me to?"

If wanting made any difference, she'd never stopped. "Yes."

He exhaled, a long shaky breath, like a weight lifter lowering a too-heavy barbell. "How?"

She shrugged, her smile almost carefree, her head tilted rakishly. "I'm open to suggestion."

"Aside from taking you in my arms and loving you until this elevator rusts around us, I can't think of any other way."

"Sex? The ultimate problem-solver?"

"Guess not," he agreed reluctantly. "If sex solved anything, we'd have no problems at all."

Color rose beneath the golden tones of her skin. Tony felt the same heat rising in him. He approached her, one step at a time. Taking her face in his hands, he kissed her with as much banked passion as he dared. Heat flared; the floor seemed to tremble.

She took his tongue into her mouth, tasting, treasuring. But when it came time to breathe again, it was Sara who held her lips away from his. "I'm sorry if all I did was talk about the baby."

"You needed to. It just made me feel so helpless. I could never say the right thing, do the right thing. Every way I turned, I messed up."

"It was the worst thing that ever happened to us."

He would have said her leaving him was worse. Did that make him a selfish bastard? He cared about her. She cared about the baby. Some dark corner of his soul resented that. It made him feel petty, small, guilty. He felt the baby's ghost drive another wedge between them.

He dropped his hands to his sides, turning one way and then the other in the center of the elevator.

"Nothing can change what happened, Sara. Going to the counselor didn't help either."

"Are you saying we can't settle this?"

Tony's jaw ached. His head pounded. He squeezed his eyes shut, rubbing them with his fingers. *If I could bring it back, I would.* Anything to make her happy. But she wouldn't let him. Making another baby was out. She'd rebuffed him every time he'd suggested it. It finally got to the point where she turned away from him in bed, or asked him to use a condom. She didn't want his baby. She didn't want him. What in God's name was he supposed to do?

He studied her, her chestnut hair pressed to the mirror. Despite the weight she claimed to have gained, her face looked thinner. A tired look smudged crescents beneath her eyes. Her unhappiness tormented him. He felt clumsy, impotent, worthless. From there to angry and alone was a path he knew well. If he could only say the right thing, make the right move. But he'd failed her. And the marriage had fallen apart.

He cleared his throat, the rusty sound reverberating in the silent elevator. "Like stepping into a minefield, isn't it?"

Her husky laugh hurt to listen to. Damned if he didn't want to reach over there and drag her into his arms and *make* it better. But how?

"If the miscarriage broke us up, we'd have to talk about it," she said cautiously.

He shrugged his shoulders. The pain was like a knife sticking in his back. "If the marriage was strong enough, one thing wouldn't have broken it up."

"You think there were other problems?"

He couldn't think of any.

She gestured in return, imitating the tilt of his head, the one-shouldered shrug. "So?"

Tony kneaded the back of his neck. Nobody had said this would be easy. But if he lost this argument, he'd lose Sara. It was too big a risk. He didn't seem to have any alternative.

His arms hung at his sides. He shook them out, loosening up his back. "What if by focusing on that one problem, we overlooked something else?"

"What else?"

"I don't know. We'd have to look for it."

Another wary silence. They listened to other cars creaking by. Other cables ran smoothly. Theirs was the one that frayed, the brakes skidding them to a halt in midair, unable to go up or down.

She studied the fingers loosely linked before her, unconsciously spinning her wedding ring around and around. "If the marriage wasn't as good as we thought, it would be better to face it now. Otherwise we'll always wonder what went wrong." After they signed the papers, she meant.

Tony kicked his sport coat out of the way and sat against the wall to her right. "I know you think it was the miscarriage; we went over that. There must have been something else, something we didn't see."

"Because I was too busy focusing on the baby."

"Because we got off track. I say we go back and find out where we went wrong."

She looked down again, her lashes casting spidery shadows on pale cheeks. "I thought we were happy."

We were, he wanted to shout. "One thing shouldn't be able to break up a happy marriage."

It can if it's as important as a baby, Sara thought.

Her hands shook slightly. She folded them tightly together.

In the months before they'd broken up, she'd begged Tony to talk to her. At last he was willing. Maybe there had been flaws in their marriage, problem areas they'd overlooked. He might be right, maybe the strain of the miscarriage fell on unseen fault lines, weaknesses they'd never examined.

She looked at him, the lean handsome face she'd loved so long. For his sake and hers, she'd take one more leap over the abyss. Maybe this time they'd land on the other side. "Okay, let's talk."

They went all the way back to the beginning.

"The day we met?" Tony repeated in surprise when she announced their first topic.

"When it comes to the important things in life, it pays to be thorough. You're saying we weren't as happy as we thought we were. If we had problems, it's better to face them now than go on pretending they didn't exist."

"Yes, ma'am," he murmured.

Her indignant glance caught his teasing smile. "Am I being officious?"

"A bit."

In that case, Sara decided, she'd keep her notepad in her briefcase—for now.

Tony sat and stretched his legs toward the center of the car, plucking at the crease in his slacks. Sara resettled herself against the middle of the back wall, her legs curled protectively under her. Her hand swept up and down her ankle, gliding along the nylon.

Their problem, she thought, was like this nylon:

transparent, tissue thin, but coloring everything beneath it. "We're total opposites, personality-wise."

"We knew that from day one."

"You're volatile. Hotheaded. Easily set off."

He threw up his hands. "I'm Italian. What can I say?"

"I'm methodical and goal-oriented."

"I'm impulsive. Or so you're always telling me."

"You don't set a lot of goals."

"I thought loving you for a lifetime was a good one."

She thanked and scolded him with the same smile. "Can we stick to the subject?"

"Love? Differences? Or loving each other's differences?"

"We were wrong for each other from day one."

"Didn't stop you from falling in love with me."

"Not that very day."

He grinned and snapped his fingers. "Just like that."

She bridled. "I did not."

"Did too."

"Did not."

"Did too."

She cast a suffering glance at the ceiling, absently brushing the folds of her blouse. She remembered the first day she met him as if it were yesterday. In real life yesterday was a numb blur. She'd plowed through her caseload, shuffling one tenant complaint after another across her desk, trying her best to prepare herself for the divorce signing. Nothing had prepared her for meeting Tony Paretti.

"I thought you were kind of cute," she admitted grudgingly.

"You thought I was perfect."

She laughed. "Hardly. You were cocky and talented and didn't give a damn about the class we were taking."

"I was too busy studying your hair and leaning forward to sniff your perfume."

"We were total opposites. I'm a hard worker."

"Too hard. You should enjoy life more." It was practically his motto. From the day they met, he'd been determined to make her life happy.

And she'd been determined to keep his organized and in focus. "You got that job on the college paper because a fraternity brother recommended you as a joke. You can't get more haphazard than that."

"It all worked out."

"Sure, but that doesn't mean the rest of life is that easy. You turned out one column after another and were an instant hit."

"People play games for a living; I get paid to write about them. Easy."

"You're a fake too."

"Hey."

"I know how hard you really work, the travel, the hours, the deadlines. You only pretend it's easy."

"That's the second time today you've defended me, *cara*. Be careful, or I'll think you still love me."

She scowled at the brushed swirls of the door. "Go ahead, act nonchalant. Pretend nothing matters—"

"Except you."

"And your romantic notions."

"Without romance, passion, and love, life isn't worth living. Let it happen, *cara*."

"A marriage has to be worked at."

"A love affair has to be enjoyed. And relished. And cherished." His gaze fixed on hers, drawing along her lips, caressing the slope of her cheek.

"Let's stick to the subject, please."

He made a move to sit up straighter. Sara practically dove for her briefcase, ticking over the combination lock with her thumbs. One, one, seven, or January 17, their wedding anniversary. One day from today, she realized, going still inside.

"Sara?"

His voice startled her back into action. Notepad in hand, she continued. "Your column made you a campus star. People quoted you. Girls ran after you."

"Including you."

"Hardly."

"Not the way I remember it. You showed up in class every day."

"I had perfect attendance. You were the one popping up behind me like a doppelganger."

He congratulated himself with a smirk. "You wanted to be there. With your brain you didn't need to attend every class."

"I'm responsible to the point of drudgery, and you know it."

"Anything you say, *cara*."

Sara made a grid on her notepad, furiously remembering. By her senior year in college she'd had her nose to the grindstone so long, it was a wonder she wasn't cross-eyed. Graduating law school at twenty-one to help impoverished tenants versus greedy landlords was such a worthy goal, she'd never questioned how much fun she'd missed in the meantime. Until a cocky underclassman named Paretti cruised into her life.

Tony brought spontaneity and fun wherever he

went. He took her on spur-of-the-moment escapades that threatened her perfect grade point average. Could spice be happy with stability? Could romantic impulsiveness ever fuse with sober responsibility?

On the other hand, he'd been what she needed, freeing a sensual, explorative nature she'd never suspected she possessed, a passion that blossomed only with him.

She glanced surreptitiously at her daydreaming husband. His dark eyes were twinkling with long-ago memories. "What are you thinking?" she asked.

"Just remembering an afternoon at Carnegie Hall. Pavarotti, anyone?"

Feeling good and guilty about skipping class, rationalizing it as "culture," she'd flipped through the program, scanning the list of arias Pavarotti would sing. Sara liked to know what lay ahead.

Then Tony Paretti sidled into the seat next to her, bumping her knees with his. "Hi. You're Sara Cohen, aren't you?"

A simple "Hi" was the extent of her tongue-tied response. A deep breath steadied her ricocheting heartbeat, bringing with it a lungful of sinfully seductive cologne. She stared at the smooth slope of his cheek, the ridge of a chiseled cheekbone.

"You may have noticed I've been sitting behind you in Foster's class every day."

Noticed? The man was sexier than a dozen Mel Gibsons and more sincere than a Hallmark greeting card. "Uh, yes. It's a good class, isn't it?"

He shrugged, giving her a dazzling smile. His wink turned her ability to breathe off and on like a light switch.

He leaned toward her, his elbow brushing perilously close to her breast. "I just wanted you to know—" *He paused, distracted by her tongue darting out to wet her lips.*

"Yes?"

"I wanted you to know I didn't follow you here."

Her eyes darted back to the program. A blush flooded her cheeks. "Of course not." *Relief and shockingly bald disappointment spiraled through her. She hadn't really expected someone that handsome, that offhandedly charming, to pay attention to her, had she?*

"You like Pavarotti," *he observed.*

"My family's always appreciated good music."

"Mine lives it."

Waiting for the program to begin, he regaled Sara with a list of Italian tenors going back two centuries. The more scandalous their exploits, the better he remembered them, drawing out detail after titillating detail. His gift for storytelling came naturally; so did his charm.

Sara, on the other hand, dryly recited the historical chronology of every piece on the program. Suffocatingly earnest and polite, she hoped to prove to the cocky Mr. Paretti that under no circumstances was she flirting.

That didn't stop her from spending the entire intermission furiously primping in the ladies' room. "This isn't a date," *she hissed into the ornate mirrors.* "He bumped into you, that's all. He's being nice."

When he volunteered to walk her home, she should have guessed he was a good deal more than that. But with the tenacity of a girl who hadn't had a date in a year and a half, she ruthlessly refused to believe in anything as glamorous as love at first sight. Lust, infatuation, stardust maybe. But love? Not with confirmed bookworm Sara Cohen.

They walked, the miles melting away as Tony's opera stories became New York stories, then Little Italy stories.

Sara walked slower and slower, convinced he'd clam up or flee when they reached her parents' imposing brownstone. He did neither. Two live-in servants and a mahogany-lined entryway failed to intimidate him. He was as matter-of-factly proud of his working-class heritage as she was subdued about her family's wealth. She noticed a depth to him that went beyond good looks and breezy charm and wished—

But wishes were for the perky blondes Mr. Paretti squired around campus.

After brief introductions her parents retired to the study. Tony edged onto the stoop. Just as Sara was about to close the door on her unrealizable fantasies, he gripped her hand and tugged her outside. She'd stood beneath the fanlight, light-headed, alarmed, expecting a good-night kiss, fortifying herself in case it never happened, reminding herself sternly that this hadn't been a date in any way, shape, or form.

He proved all her doubts correct, stepping to the sidewalk without so much as a good-bye. She'd been a bore, her conscience shouted, a drone with a sheaf of papers for a heart. He was going!

Then he turned, sweeping her a bow from the sidewalk. He proceeded to warble Pavarotti's final aria as a farewell, singing so badly, so horrendously off-key, but with such gusto and sheer uninhibited bravado, Sara nearly choked with laughter.

Tony finished on a high note that broke neatly in two, then turned his palms up in a classic so-sue-me shrug. He waited for her response.

He was trying to make an impression, she realized with a shock that resounded through the years. He'd made a play for her approval. He actually cared what she thought.

She fell in love on the spot.

SIX

"I thought you'd waltz off down the street after your aria," she commented in the elevator.

Tony grinned, adding his own memories. "I asked if I could call you."

"You asked me my name. For the fifth time. You kept pretending you'd forgotten it."

"Because every time I did, you got this wide-eyed look, as if you believed I really would."

"I was very insecure."

"I couldn't believe you'd think I'd forget you that quick, *cara*."

"Other guys had."

"Ah," he murmured. "The truth comes out."

She shrugged, making a show of total unconcern. "I never pretended to be the most popular girl on campus."

"Nor were you as bespectacled and boring as you like to think. You were fascinating, warm, funny, smarter than heck. You intimidated the pants off me."

She forced a wry smile. "Intimidating men isn't the easiest way to get a date."

"Good thing I liked a challenge."

"And when the challenge was over?" She watched him purse his lips, a knowing smile flickering there.

"I was hooked."

Her heart quivered. Embers warmed her chest when his eyes darkened. Chocolate, she thought, he had eyes the color of melting chocolate. They'd melted her heart.

She squinted at the ceiling, tapping her blank notepad with the capped end of a ballpoint pen. "I think it was your singing I fell in love with first."

He blinked, shocked out of a deeply held conviction he could charm birds from trees—but not with his voice. "My singing?! I can't sing worth a damn."

"So you demonstrated. I thought you were sweet."

"It wasn't a bid for pity!" He folded his arms, crossing his outstretched legs at the ankles. "My singing," he muttered with disgust.

"Well, it certainly wasn't your looks," she retorted with a dry chuckle. "They were a major factor against you. You were so dashing, I never thought I'd have a chance."

He had movie-star looks and he knew it. But to his credit, his looks, like his writing talent, were something he usually took for granted. Unlike most vain men, he never worked at his appearance.

Closing her eyes, grinning, Sara returned to their shared memory. "You stopped singing eventually," she murmured.

"The neighbors were probably grateful."

His song finished, their laughter ended, she'd rapidly gotten her hopes under control and shoved her heart back onto the shelf like a textbook.

He'd astonished her by taking the stairs two at a time, pausing inches away. His palms cupped her face as if he couldn't believe he held something so precious, or dared steal something as coveted as a kiss. His lips found hers, capturing and disclosing, revealing a pact between them she'd never suspected nor sought. Love wasn't something they'd built over time, it was something they discovered in one heart-dancing moment.

Sara opened her eyes to find him watching her as he had that night, waiting for her reaction.

"What are you thinking?" he asked.

"That it was all so sudden. And yet it seemed so permanent. As if it had always been there."

He nodded, reliving the instant bond.

"We'd only had that one accidental date," she argued.

He shook his head, sexy and sure. "You were mine the minute I touched you."

She huffed. "If egos were balloons, Paretti, you'd be the *Hindenburg*."

"It happens fast sometimes."

"The way a bubble bursts?"

"The way a parachute deploys. They don't call it falling in love for nothing. We fell together. And love caught us."

"Like in this elevator?"

Ping.

They both looked up, Sara *tsk*ing at the aptness of the sound effect. The light over the number panel blinked. Staticky music floated in from hidden speakers. "Some Enchanted Evening."

Tony scooted over beside her. She made room for him, untucking her legs alongside his, rationalizing that they'd been falling asleep anyway. Sparks and needles prickled up and down her calves. Other unnameable sensations tingled down the side of her neck as Tony leaned over and whispered, "They're playing our song."

She scowled, plucking at the hem of her skirt. She crossed her right leg over her left, creating a safety zone between his leg and hers. "This was never our song."

"It could have been."

She sighed. Every time she tried to be reasonable, he resorted to starry-eyed optimism. Tony was a romantic and a sensualist. She shouldn't forget that. As he edged closer, his thigh nudging hers, she searched in vain for the briefcase to set between them as a barrier. She couldn't reach it, not with his arm insinuating itself between her lower back and the wall.

He tugged her to him with insistent tenderness, oblivious to her slight resistance. Guilt plagued her. He was a good man, wonderfully funny and tender, infuriating and intense. Stubborn, she had to remember stubborn—

Tony watched her eyes cloud over, a tiny furrow of worry on her brow. His jaw clenched. He held on; holding on to her was what this was all about. As long as he kept on touching her, he could overlook how much it hurt when she braced herself against him.

Their first date may have been a long time ago, but the courage to love someone never changed. He thought of the contortions he'd gone through working up his courage to approach the frizzy-haired girl with the dazzling darting eyes, the fierce intelligence, the shy smile. Then he'd bumped into her at the concert and decided to go for broke.

Sometimes jumping in with both feet was the only answer. If he wanted her to remember how much they'd once loved each other, he had to remind her how much of it was physical. Love was expressed in a lot of ways, some more explicit than others. "Remember that afternoon at Frank's loft?"

She stiffened beside him. "Why bring that up?"

"We're going back to the beginning, aren't we? It was our first time. Should show how compatible we were."

She wrinkled her nose at the banal term. "Compatible?"

If he'd said anything stronger, she'd have lurched out of his arms, seeking the sanctuary of a distant corner. He played it light, fighting his instincts every inch of the way. He brushed his nose against her hair, dragging in the scent of her shampoo. A musky aroma hid in the swirling depths of her curls. He wanted to dive in after it.

"We fit," he murmured. "You and I. You were nervous." *Like now.*

She tugged her fingers through the winding strands of her hair. They bounced back, bobbing in the faint breeze of his breath. "I was worried."

"Did you think we were wrong for each other?"

"We were a total mismatch." She practically pleaded with him to agree.

He did. To a point. "You're focused. I let things flow. You have to know in what direction and at what speed. But none of that mattered when we came together. We set our own speed."

He gripped her fingers as he spoke. "Your hand fit mine as we walked up the stairs to the loft. I didn't let go until I had to, digging through my pockets for the key Frank had loaned me. Your lips fit mine as we sat on the edge of the mattress. Your breast fit my palm—"

He raised her palm to his lips, planting a soft kiss there, sensing more than hearing her intake of breath.

"Don't," she whispered, closing her palm over his kiss as if capturing a butterfly.

"It was good."

"I never said loving you was the problem. There were other things—"

"None of them as important as that. Do you love me, Sara?"

They held very still. Her gaze locked on the opposite wall.

"Do you?"

"We can't live together," she said at last.

She hadn't denied it, Tony told himself. His lawyer wife hadn't denied she loved him still.

He took a deep breath, let it ache, then let it out. Had it been this hard the first time? This scary?

In the loft she'd said she loved him for the first time. He took her there again. Now she thought they were searching for faults in their early years, an issue that might have broken them apart.

Tony had his own agenda. He'd show her the good times instead, balancing out the bad. He'd prove to her that one awful event couldn't erase ten incredible years. He'd show her exactly how compatible they were.

"I couldn't get enough of you that day, Sara." Nor all the days since. "You were hot, your skin on fire for me. We almost sizzled together."

She huffed a silent laugh, the tension easing in her shoulders. She murmured a familiar refrain. "I knew I shouldn't have married a writer."

"Let me do it with words. We can't do it any other way. Not here."

"No, we can't."

He heard the husky tone of her voice and held himself back by sheer force of will. He couldn't rush this, no matter how many times he caught her glancing at the paneling, shifting her nylon-encased legs on the carpet. She drew them up slightly. He leaned onto one hip, easing closer. He talked on, painting her a picture, hazy and erotic, his murmuring baritone reverberating in the tiny room.

Sara sank against his chest, his voice's vibration rumbling against her arm, the warm musky scent of him evoking memories, even stronger realities. She fought a growing lethargy, an underlying restlessness. They were talking about the past, trying to uncover the faults that had brought them to this place, looking for problems. *And finding nothing but love.*

She steeled herself against the memories, the achy, insinuating impressions they created. She listened to the rise and fall of his voice. Words were so intimate. They entered you, gliding into your brain, creating pictures, responses. She'd loved his voice as long as she'd loved his body.

He'd called home every night when he was on the road. She'd lie in bed listening to his voice. He never failed to say he loved her, and missed her.

She'd missed him this last year. And loved him. The wayward, unanchored feeling that had swirled around her since their breakup, evaporated when he moved nearer, replaced by something tangible.

Without realizing it, she burrowed closer, listening to his midnight whisper, the two of them linked by memories instead of phone lines.

"We touched," he murmured, going back to the first time. "I unbuttoned your blouse. You put your fingertips on my belt buckle. I didn't think I'd last past that. Then you lifted my shirt and kissed my chest. I practically exploded. So did you. You went wild. Clinging to me, kissing me, wrapping your arms around me, and your legs."

Sara blushed. She'd hoped speed would make up for fear. "I was trying to keep up with you."

"You turned me on faster than a light switch. I thought I'd die if I couldn't have you right then and there."

"But we didn't—"

"No. We didn't do it right then." Tony raised his arm from her waist to her shoulders, the better to nestle her head in the crook of his arm. His other hand reached for hers, bringing the back of it to his thigh, cradling her palm against his. Their fingers twined slowly like the first time they made love. Sara remembered it plainly.

They'd climbed the four stories to Frank's loft, her knees trembling every step of the way. The importance of what they were about to do filled her with doubts. What would she say when he discovered she was a virgin? The possibility that he'd already guessed mortified her. Tony was gorgeous, charming, experienced. Focusing on how much she wanted him filled her with searing desire and jittery nerves.

He'd accepted her fevered caresses with intensity of his own. They'd tumbled to the bed in a blaze of tangled limbs and inarticulate moans. But love wasn't only about passion. He soon showed her how much more it could be.

Love was tenderness, excruciating gentleness, delicate persistent exploration. He uncovered her shyness, peeling away layers of specially bought silk underthings as if they were nothing but wrapping and camouflage. Which they were.

She'd shuddered at his knowingness, the intuition that led him to her most sensitive spots. She'd thought it would be give and take, his leg between hers, her hand closing around him, one's pleasure, then the other's.

They did everything together, opening the condom, making it a game. When her fingers slid over him, his taut anticipation revealed the power she held.

Sensation superseded technique. His excitement fed hers. She stopped focusing on what to do and began living it. When he thrust slowly into her, she knew they'd found the most perfect possible expression of love. It rose on a tide of tiny cries, spiraling in ever tighter circles, ending with a whirlpool of eddying sensations flooding outward, rippling through her veins, seeping from her eyes in tears of awe.

In the elevator the carpet itched, the air grew musty. Sara shifted her weight and discovered how close she and Tony had become. Her cheeks grew warm as she realized how her fingers vined with his, reminiscent of two lovers lying side by side, exhausted and exhilarated by an afternoon of love, their bodies lightly sheened with sweat.

"Remember the rain?" he asked. His voice sounded rusty. "On the windowpanes above us?"

She brought her hands firmly together in her lap, drying one on her skirt, hoping to heaven he hadn't noticed. They were searching for faults, yet everything he'd described seemed so right. "Mm. That rain."

"It trickled down like your tears. I licked them away. Remember?"

She clamped her eyes shut. "I wasn't upset."

"I thought I'd hurt you. You scared me."

She swung around, wide-eyed. "You knew exactly what you were doing."

"You didn't." He laughed, then grew quiet, brushing a lock of hair from her temple, tangling his finger in it. "I was terrified I'd hurt you."

"It's supposed to hurt a little."

"But this was you and me. I wanted it to be perfect. Especially for you."

A tear gathered at the corner of Sara's lashes. She blinked it away. Did he have to be so typically Tony? He always took such elaborate care of her, putting her feelings ahead of his own. What woman in her right mind would let a man like that get away? She disguised a sniff. "You brought me a washcloth, or tried."

"You wouldn't let me get up."

"I didn't want to let you go."

"Why now?"

She shot him a look, the spell broken.

Tony cursed and sat back, instantly regretting the words. It was enough she was willing to talk. He shouldn't have pushed it.

They both rearranged themselves on the floor. His heels stretched toward the panel. Sara's stretched toward the opposite corner. She bounced her knees slightly. "Falling asleep," she explained.

It was time Tony woke her up. "We had it good for a lot of years."

"It was."

He noticed the past tense too. "Does that mean it's over?"

"If it was, we wouldn't be talking."

Tony swallowed the sharp lump in his throat. Sometimes it hurt more to hope than to simply give up. Sheer stubbornness, and a love he couldn't deny, wouldn't let him. "Do you want to stay married to me?"

"I don't know how we can."

The quieter her voice got, the louder his became. "Do you want to?" So help him, he practically shook her.

Her head bobbed. Her eyes brimmed. "Yes. I always wanted to."

Tony dragged her into his arms. "Just don't let it go," he whispered starkly. "We'll figure out a way. We can *make* it work."

"We tried so hard."

"Keep trying, dammit. We'll talk."

"We talked."

"We'll listen better."

"We listened."

"We'll care."

She drew back.

His heart grew still, his throat dry.

"I still care, Tony."

"So do I." He pressed his mouth to hers, hungrily, everything he needed inside her.

She yielded, her body bending to his like a willow. Their tongues met, caressed. Their breath mingled. Urgency gripped them. So much time to make up for. So many things unsaid, unsayable.

Only touch communicated how deeply he'd missed her. Only surrender conveyed his sorrow. He knew words would never encompass it. But a dam broke and the words poured out. "I'm so sorry," he whispered over and over.

"So am I."

"God, I needed you. It never stopped. I wanted you every day since we broke up. To talk, to hold you."

"Don't let it happen again."

"We'll find a way out."

"I love you."

"I love you."

He lifted her chin, his fingertips splayed along the column of her throat. She stretched toward him. He read the questions in her eyes. Going back into the past proved how much they'd once loved. But what about the future? What happened next?

One step at a time, he thought, answering her silence with kisses. Her lips trembled, parted. He put his tongue between them, reliving the gentle easing way he'd first entered her. When he could speak, he said, "Let's just remember how good it was."

"And everything else?"

"We'll get there."

For now he wanted to hold her, that was all.

Sara had other ideas. She led his hand to her breast, hurrying. His Sara always hurried when the itch for his touch grew too strong. She sipped at his tongue-tip, forming her mouth to accept him. Slipping his tongue inside, he made love to her mouth, another beginning.

With a groan she raised her arms around his neck. "Kiss me. Please."

He gripped her so tight, he thought he'd hurt her if he didn't pull back. She sensed his withdrawal.

Her mouth curved in a sultry arc, familiar and teasing. "I'm small, not fragile."

His hand nearly spanned her lower back. She let him press her toward him, her breasts skimming his chest.

His stomach clenched, instantly tight. She sensed that, too, flattening her palm against his rippling muscles, slipping her fingers inside his belt. They'd tangoed on this cliff edge so many times, she knew exactly what to do.

Why had they ever tried to talk this out? Tony wondered. Love that burned this hot was always right. He knew her body and soul. That's what made it so hard to walk away.

A flick of his tongue trailed the side of her neck, a bite. She gasped and craned to be nearer, flaming at the feel of his palm gripping her hip. He slid her downward until they reclined on the elevator floor, thigh to thigh, mouth to mouth. "Open your eyes," he whispered "Look at me."

Her gaze met his, filled with banished doubts, unspoken urgency. Tony dawdled, drawing the moment out to a tantalizing eternity. The corner of his mouth crooked in a smile. He'd always loved the way her eyes misted with desire, the way they grew wide with wonder when his hand trespassed across her breast. They would drift love-shut when he filled her.

Soon.

He unfastened her skirt, snicking open a garter with a deft move of his thumb. He couldn't risk waiting. He raked the side of her neck with a vicious kiss. She arched into him until he groaned. "Do you want this?"

"I want you."

The words nearly undid him. His hand found her raised knee, his finger teasing the sensitive underside. She gripped his finger there until he slid it out. Escaping to fondle the outside of her thigh, he grazed the strip of bare heated skin above the rim of her nylons.

A dizzy sensation raced through his veins. Maneuvering, he kicked the door with his heel.

The thump distracted her. Her eyes cleared, then grew cloudy once more, focusing on rising desires. He kissed them closed, inching her body beneath him.

He drew the lapels of her blouse open, revealing silk and lace. He let his teeth drag the frail cup downward.

Another thud. It could have been his heart.

"Tony?"

He accepted her papery whisper. His throat burned too.

"Tony."

He recognized that halting tone. He ignored it. They were so close to connecting, to repairing the damage—

"Get up." She hissed as if the elevator were on fire, rapping his back with her fists for good measure.

He rolled off her. Wriggling furiously into a corner, she fumbled with her blouse.

"What'd I say?"

"We've got company," she replied.

He glanced up. Three stories above them silhouettes wavered in a square of light. The thud of a workboot on the roof made Tony curse. He leapt to his feet faster than a base runner called out after a headfirst slide into home plate. "Who's up there?"

"Ms. Cohen? Mr. Paretti? Are you there please?" A mocking insinuation threaded itself through Melchior's voice.

Sara rolled her eyes. "Of course we're here, Michael. Where else would we be? And what else would we be doing?" she added with a disgusted mutter. "I can't believe I let you talk me into that."

"Pardon me?" Melchior asked.

"Yes, we're here," she shouted. From her refuge in the corner she bent slightly forward, peering up at the opening.

Tony muttered his own choice expletive. "You'd think people could find some privacy in an elevator. Next time we close that damn vent."

"Who says there'll be a next time?" She'd meant it as a retort. The sudden vision of spending the rest of her life without him made Sara ache. One kiss from him and she'd been back in that loft, loving the only man she'd ever loved, forgiving everything, forgetting everything. They'd been a part of each other's lives so long.

But she had to be sensible. Having sex in elevators

wasn't about to solve their problems. Let him seduce her with his touch, and she'd agree to anything. Let him kiss her again, and her heart would say yes, forever.

She fixed her mouth in a frown, the better to discuss matters with Michael. If they were about to get out, she had a decision to make. Did she sign those papers or give the two of them one more try? Had they even begun to solve what separated them?

"Are we rescued, Michael?" she called.

"Not yet," he replied. "That's why we've sent this gift, a show of our good faith and best efforts to make you comfortable during your stay. Compliments of Melchior, Kravitz, and Keene." A wicker picnic basket tottered into view, thumping the roof of the elevator.

Tony grinned at Sara's terse and very salty response. He egged her on with a wink. "Tell him what you think of that."

She had enough scowls to go around. The first she bestowed on Tony as he sauntered into the corner. "We'd rather get out of here if it's all the same with you," she shouted. She missed his flinch.

So that's what she wanted, Tony thought. To get to those offices and sign those papers. Frustration ate at him. He spared a glance in the mirror for the Latin lover who never could manage to keep discussions with his logical wife on a purely platonic plane. Oh no. He had to wrap her in his arms, kiss her until she gasped and writhed, overplay his hand until he scared her straight into Melchior's office.

He watched her now, fidgeting with her blouse while the engineer shouted down more excuses why they had to stay another couple of hours. When

Melchior threw in his two cents' worth, she snuck her hand behind her to tug on her skirt. Balancing on one foot, she tiptoed the other backward, searching blindly for her shoe. She found the strap and dragged it over, stepping up onto the stiletto heel while nodding at everything her lawyer said.

Tony backed into the corner and cursed himself. His passion in the face of her prudence had always been his downfall. He couldn't win her back that way. Sara followed her feelings only so far. She had to *know* what was going on. He couldn't tell her. All he honestly knew was that he loved her. And it wasn't enough.

SEVEN

The basket thumped again. Tony mentally compared how many times he'd kicked the door with how many times he'd heard that thud. Sara's cheeks were red enough without telling her how long their rescuers had tried to get their attention.

"Can you retrieve that?" Melchior asked.

Tony grunted, eyeing the opening. He came up beside Sara, his body skimming hers. She quickly got out of the way. He lowered his gaze and his voice. "When they're gone, we can pick up where we left off."

"No, Tony." She couldn't make it much plainer than that. But her pale olive complexion said otherwise, embers glowing in her cheeks. Her chest rose and fell with panted breaths. Her nipples remained peaked.

Tony almost tasted the pebbled flesh. "Making love *is* communicating."

"We stick to sensible discussion, or I climb out of here on that rope."

He scoffed at her idea of a rope. The basket dangled on transparent monofilament line, the kind he'd used tarpon fishing off the Florida coast. He heard the ratcheting whir of a reel as Melchior played the line out and wondered vaguely where they'd gotten the pole.

The basket obliterated the view, bouncing in the opening. Tony thought fast and hard. He'd gotten Sara to admit she loved him by reigniting a passion that hadn't completely died. But love, especially married love, had to extend beyond the bedroom. They had other things to discuss, provided they had time.

"Okay, lower it again," he yelled. The edge just caught. Tony leapt and tipped it, guiding it through the hole. "See?" he said to Sara, "even Michael Jordan would be happy to make this basket."

She groaned.

Tony lowered it to the floor. Inside, glass clinked and weight shifted. Retrieving his army knife, Tony severed the monofilament. "Take 'er up," he called.

The line disappeared through the ceiling. Tony squinted at the gift card tucked into a floppy plaid bow tied around the basket's handle. "Cute idea."

"It's primarily for Sara," Melchior announced. "We pride ourselves on highly personalized service to our clients. Are you all right, Sara dear?"

Tony shot a glance her way. Relieved to be out of the spotlight, she bustled through her briefcase, retrieving lipstick and a comb. "I'm fine," she shouted.

Not from what Tony knew of her voice she wasn't. She was embarrassed. Tony wondered what their small audience had seen and honestly didn't care. In fact, a purely male, completely Neanderthal surge of pride pounded through him. Possessiveness puffed his chest. Let Melchior keep that in mind; Sara was *his*.

Practically bumping her nose against the mirror, Sara hastily reapplied the lip liner Tony had kissed off.

"Think you can undo everything we just did?" Tony asked softly.

She saved her scowl for the mirror. "A couple of hours did you say, Mr. Scott?"

"At least," the engineer answered. "The problem is in the cable control on the top floor."

Presentable at last, Sara inched into the center of the car. With a false but hearty wave, she signaled Melchior. "See you later, then."

"Enjoy your—lunch—my dear."

Before the doors above hushed shut, Tony grabbed the displaced ceiling tile and hefted it overhead. "They'll have to knock next time."

"I think they did," she answered, paying more attention to the reorganization of her cosmetics case than his efforts to wedge the acoustic tile back in place.

Job done, he rested his hands on his waist, staring at the ceiling.

"How much do you think they saw?" she asked quietly.

"There was a time you wouldn't have cared."

"I've always hated being embarrassed, and you know it."

"They saw."

She huffed and turned back to the mirror.

"Who's the mask for this time?" he asked.

She refused to meet his gaze. Retrieving a compact, she pattered a haze of powder across her flaming cheekbones. "I knew I shouldn't have worn rouge."

"That isn't rouge."

"How would you know?" Pat, pat, pat.

"Because I put it there. You were hot for me."

"I'm always hot. It's my metabolism."

He shook his head. "Pure sex and you know it."

"So you like to think."

"So you can't deny." She'd certainly never convince him by dancing around the elevator like an anxious schoolgirl on a first date.

He'd gotten to her, Tony thought. She might want to run, but fate gave her no place to hide. She had to deal with him.

"What's in the basket anyway?" She plopped herself down, eagerly poking through her new briefcase substitute.

"Food always did take precedence over me," Tony grumbled.

Laughing in agreement, she reached into the basket and waggled a tiny jar in his direction. "Beluga caviar? You haven't got a chance."

"We'll see."

"First we'll eat." She tugged out a bottle of red wine. Two glasses followed, then a collection of baby-sized jars of jams and pâtés, and wrapped columns of imported crackers. Small knives and spoons were nestled in straw toward the bottom, too delicate to be real.

She shook her head, reading the label on a red circle of Dutch cheese. "I can't believe Michael did this."

"Wonderful, isn't he?"

"As a matter of fact—" She stopped in mid-sentence, suddenly engrossed in the label on another foil-wrapped cheese.

Tony started to ask what else. His heart completed the sentence for him. A clammy breeze out of nowhere chilled his skin. His blood slowed to a rusty faucet's drip.

Michael, she'd called him. Not Mr. Melchior.

Nonsense, he silently insisted, clinging to her kind of logic. The man was her lawyer, not her lover.

Tony burned a gaze right through the crooked ceiling tile, trying to remember what this *Michael* looked like. Melchior's oily voice echoed in the abyss surrounding them. *We pride ourselves on highly personalized service to our clients.*

Highly personalized Tony's foot. Had he been "servicing" Sara?

She set out two gold-rimmed plates, avoiding his look with each new item, hiding an embarrassed flush. He was her husband; what could possibly embarrass her around him?

"Say cheese." She waved a wedge of Brie at him.

He rubbed a hand across his mouth. The gnawing in his gut wasn't hunger anymore.

He paced, trying desperately to quell the whole crazy idea. If he had one bad quality, besides impulsiveness, possessiveness, and unchecked passion, it was old-fashioned, all-consuming, green-as-grass jealousy. He'd married Sara because she was steady as a rock, deeply committed to anything she put her mind to. He'd never doubted her for a moment.

It was him he doubted. Deep down he'd always suspected she could do better than a lanky sports-writer with bad taste in ties. Maybe she preferred a top-notch lawyer with a suite of top-floor offices. Somebody who gave out gold-rimmed china plates in wicker picnic baskets for Christmas gifts, instead of last year's Super Bowl souvenirs.

"Did you eat?" she asked pleasantly.

"I forced down a bowl of oatmeal this morning at Ma's. I didn't want to hurt her feelings."

That earned him a grin, a softly understanding gaze that quickly reverted to the basket. "You take very good care of her."

"That's what you do with people you love."

She didn't answer, too busy chuckling at the linen napkins clamped inside the basket's top. "A miniature tablecloth!" She flapped it out until it formed a three-by-three-foot square in their paneled aerie. "Michael does travel in style."

Tony swallowed a shot of acid. He didn't want to hear it. Part of him clung to a well-known fact; jealousy was the stupidest of emotions. His own insecurity made him think this stuff.

They'd been separated a year. Who's to say she hadn't found another man? Any guy with eyes in his head would see what a treasure she was.

The gourmet lunch looked less appetizing by the minute. Sara set the jars in methodical rows, along with the crackers, dried fruits, and desserts. Then she set to work on the cheeses, slicing, arranging, spreading.

The coins in Tony's pockets jangled like his nerves. Sara, he thought, whispering her name to himself like a prayer. If she'd found another man, whose fault was it?

"Sit down," she chirped, reaching for the wine. "Uh-oh. They didn't give us a corkscrew."

"You mean Michael messed up?"

She blithely ignored his sarcasm.

Tony crouched and took the bottle from her. Melchior had messed up all right. He'd left Tony alone with Sara. Sexist and old-fashioned as it might be, nothing made his blood race like the prospect of a rival. And nothing sapped his confidence like the idea of Sara loving someone else.

They didn't have time for this! He had a couple of hours at best to show her how good their marriage had been. And here he sat, bedeviling himself with fantasies of her unfaithfulness.

He had to woo her back, to win her all over again. But he'd never be able to do it unless she told him what had happened during the last year. Had she been as lonely as he? Or had she found comfort with someone less temperamental, quicker to listen and sympathize? And love?

He flicked open his Swiss Army knife, cutting the bottle's seal with one neat slice. He shoved the corkscrew into the cork, spiraling downward with a twist of his wrist. "Bet Melchior doesn't carry one of these."

"Probably not."

"You're the one who's usually prepared for anything. Good thing I'm here." Clamping the bottle under his arm, he pulled the cork with an airless thump.

"Save the I-told-you-so's for after lunch." She spread the pâté on the wheat crackers, sniffing before taking a bite.

He poured the first glass of wine, waving a sample beneath his nose. Inhaling, he let the warm red aroma fill his head, tantalizing his taste buds, easing the haze of anxiety taunting him. He sipped, washing wine across his tongue, savoring it, hoping like hell that when he opened his eyes she'd be looking at him the way she had a few moments before, desire in her eyes.

He opened his eyes and saw gold. Flecks of precious metal seemed to float in the depths of her warm brown eyes. Heat kindled in her cheeks. The tip of her tongue outlined her full lips, swollen from his kisses.

"Taste good?" she asked.

The opening she handed him for a suggestive comeback was wider than the Yankees' gap in center field. Absolutely nothing came to him. He tossed back the rest of the wine, trying to chase the tension from his throat. He didn't have the guts to come right out and ask, not yet. Just because he'd opted out of every halfhearted opportunity to start up new relationships this last year didn't mean she had. She was a beautiful, intelligent, sparkling woman who knew her own worth. He liked to think he'd contributed to the last part.

He hefted the bottle and sloshed a stream of wine into her offered glass.

"Whoa." She chuckled.

"Eat, drink, and be merry. Tomorrow we may divorce."

She laughed, visibly relieved at the not-so-subtle way he'd kept his distance since the basket arrived. "You know I never drink more than half a glass."

He knew. Another lousy idea hit him with all the subtlety of a linebacker. Did anyone else know how many drinks it took to get Sara drunk? He'd been around athletes long enough to know the attitudes some men had toward women. If a woman was naive enough to let down her guard, they'd take full advantage.

His gut twisted like a Grand Prix racecourse. Sara was faithful, committed. She never gave up, whether defending clients or loving him. He'd staked his life on that. Sara was *his*. Or had been. Maybe these barbed-wire doubts were punishment for his walking out, for not having the guts to stay.

"Tony." She'd said his name at least three times. "Where on earth are you?"

He gave her a heartsick grin. "Sorry. Trying to decide what to eat first." Arsenic or strychnine.

"Why don't we start with cheese?"

Wedges of cheese and an array of crackers decorated each plate, accompanied by wafers of dried apricots and candied oranges.

"Heidi Cohen had an apt pupil," Tony said.

Sara grinned. "When it came to my mother's culinary talents, I mastered presentation only. You know I can't cook."

"We were cooking a minute ago."

She refused to bite. "Behave. First we eat. Then we get some priorities straight."

"Such as?"

"We need to talk."

The cheese turned to paste in his mouth. "Is there something you want to tell me?"

She looked at him a long time, sipping the wine, mulling over various approaches. Her eye lit on the tipping wine bottle. "You're strangling the burgundy."

His hand squeaked, clammy, shaking. "So tell me about him."

"Who?"

"The new man in your life."

"What?"

At least she looked right at him when she said it, Tony thought. He took a cracker from her hand, nibbling the caviar her lips had been about to touch. "Melchior. How involved are you?"

Sara stared at him, things slowly becoming clear. "So that's why you got so quiet. I should have recognized brooding when I didn't hear it."

"And?"

Her And Game. For all the times he'd teased her about her system for keeping the lines of communication open, he sure used it when he needed it.

Sara sipped her wine. A woman was not a man's to possess. However, that liberated thought had never quenched the strange cherished feeling she got when Tony grew possessive. "I'm not a flirt, you know that."

She'd been clumsy and inept around men—until Tony had come along and made her feel like the sexiest woman on earth. Michael, on the other hand, made her feel as if attractiveness were a social skill, something she could improve on in order to impress his fellow attorneys at company functions.

Nevertheless, she chose her words carefully. Tony's jealousy might be silly and unfounded, but she recognized its cause. He'd worked so hard to convince her she was lovable. Somehow she'd failed to convince him of the same thing. "You have nothing to be insecure about, you know."

"And him?"

She sighed. "We had a few dates."

He winced as if the wine had turned to vinegar.

"You and I were separated, Tony."

"Do you need an excuse?"

She flared at his quiet judgment. "Nothing happened. Why am I justifying myself to you? After you moved away, I thought everything was over. You acted as if you didn't give a damn about saving our marriage."

"So Melchior's my fault?"

"I did what I could to get on with my life. I went out, saw friends, and dated."

"That stuffy horse's ass?"

"A couple of others too."

"A couple of other horses' asses?" he inquired dryly.

She laughed in spite of herself, setting her fingertips on his arm. "Tony, don't torture yourself. I know what you're thinking. Until the divorce is final, I wouldn't even think of getting involved, much less having sex with someone else."

"That would make a difference to you?"

"I'm married." She looked him in the eye. Her sensitive, seething, Mediterranean man would have to accept that.

Apparently he did. Munching a plain cracker, he swirled his glass of wine, watching its burgundy depths. "You could have told me about Melchior anyway."

She drew herself up, the battle only half won. "We were separated."

He shrugged, raising his glance until it leveled off with hers, a relentless probing stare. "You could have called."

She squealed in sheer frustration. "We just went over that! I wouldn't call you until you called me—

Oh, for heaven's sake. You're the one who wanted to go to Chicago and 'start fresh.' As if I were some kind of baseball trade, exchanged for a player to be named later!"

"I'm just saying why keep this thing with Melchior secret if there was nothing going on?"

"First of all, there was no 'thing' with Melchior. Secondly, how could I have called? What would I say? 'Hi, Tony. I wanted to let you know I'm *not* dating anyone who means anything to me.'"

"It's a start."

"Right. Then I'd tell you an even bigger secret— I have none. No secrets and not much of a life. Without you I felt as if I'd gone back to square one, miserable and lonely and socially inept. I *hated* dating. I plowed into my work. I dreaded going home at night knowing you wouldn't be there, going to bed knowing you wouldn't be there, falling asleep knowing that when I woke up—"

Emotions she'd thought she had completely under control hit her from all sides. She should have been better prepared. Scanning the floor for the bottle, she downed the last of her glass of wine, recovering her composure. "You have no reason to be jealous. I've never been attracted to anyone the way I was to you."

"Still are?"

"Still am." She sighed, perplexed and dejected. "Don't ask me why."

He didn't need to. The wine did the work. No one could talk herself into a crying jag or a self-righteous oratorio faster than Sara. If he knew her, she had a whole list of what they'd missed this last year. He needed to hear it.

"Don't ask why I raced back into my shell," she repeated, pouring another drink. "Especially when one realizes—with utter clarity, mind you—I am not drunk yet—that you're the single most illogical, egotistical *meshuga* Italian in the entire five-borough area."

"I love you too."

She looked up, blinking rapidly. "What was that?"

"I love you, too, Princess."

Before she knew it, the entire elevator tilted. She gasped, her arms clamping around his neck. "Are we falling again?"

"I hope so." His mouth covered hers in a deep and none-too-gentle kiss. "He doesn't mean a thing to you, does he?"

"He who?" She gulped. The car spun. Exasperating, had she said exasperating? She had a whole list of Tony's faults backed up in her brain like airplanes circling LaGuardia.

Tony seemed to have heard nothing but praise. He kissed her again. The list grew hazy. In seconds the words began to waver and disappear, replaced with images, mesmerizing, dizzying, heated images she couldn't resist.

She tore herself away, trying to regain her balance by focusing on details. Bad strategy. His eyes were as intense as the headlights of an oncoming subway train. His cheekbones were slashes of piratical purpose. His lips— "Boy, am I drunk." She tried to sit up.

"Not as drunk as you want to be."

He knew her too well. Tipsy, she threw caution to the wind, becoming the uninhibited woman she'd always secretly wanted to be. Tipsy, she didn't have to think, to plan, to look at the long term. With Tony, the moment was enough. Moments made up life—exquisite, erotic, plundering, ravishing moments of undiluted desire. With Tony, she let go of the schedules and structures. And somehow the world righted itself without her help. Somehow things worked out. If only *they* worked out, her in his arms, Tony inside her.

Being tipsy was Sara's only hope, she realized with a flash of utter clarity. If she was the least bit drunk, he'd be a gentleman about it. Sober, she had no defense whatsoever against his grim smile, the taut lips that only softened when meeting hers, luring her into kisses that had been her undoing more times than she could count. From that first kiss on her parents' front steps, she'd known there was no one else in this world for her. . . .

He drank in the longing in her eyes, met and matched it. "Sara," he cooed. "You're not that drunk."

"Oh yes I am." Kisses weren't answers. She got lost in kisses.

Somewhere in her careening thoughts one idea came clear. Lying in the arms of her nearly-ex-husband in a stranded elevator was no way to pursue a reconciliation. Just because he cared enough to get jealous didn't mean they'd made any progress. "We have a problem."

"Do we?" He shoved the picnic basket out of the way with his foot.

"Bigger problems." She struggled to sit up. He reluctantly released her. She scooted back against the wall. "We haven't solved anything yet."

"I thought we could try."

"Not that way."

Tony poured himself the last of the wine, watching her regroup. He pursed his lips on the rim of the glass, the moisture of his breath forming an outline. "What do you suggest?"

"Before we talk anymore about the marriage, maybe we'd better talk about what happened during our separation."

"You said nothing happened."

"Not to me."

She always could pin him to the mat with a few perfectly chosen words. He developed a sudden consuming interest in apricot jam on toast squares.

"Tony?"

It was his turn to shrug.

"I know you dated."

"How?"

"I read about it."

He raised two black brows, then drew them sharply together as he studied the pâté. "You followed the column pretty closely."

She'd done everything but use a magnifying glass. "The series on sports groupies was fascinating."

Tony sighed, wiping crumbs from his hands. He reclined, stretching his legs across the elevator, and balanced on one elbow. "I didn't touch any of them."

She looked into his eyes. He knew that piercing stare. Mrs. Cohen had used it on him the first time Sara had brought him home. The see-to-the-soul look. Italians had it, too, but in his family they associated it more with collectors of bad debts.

"Okay," he said at last, "you think I had affairs with a couple of sports groupies."

"It's a couple now?"

"I interviewed them. I never touched them."

"No?"

"I held them." He saw the misgivings that little amendment caused. "Hugged." Even worse, judging from her big brown eyes. He was digging himself a hole, and he didn't even have a shovel. "They meant nothing to me."

His heart sank the minute he heard the words—the philanderer's motto and creed. While he castigated himself for the pitiful cliché, Sara launched into a frenzied cleanup. She slammed dishes into the basket, cranking lids on the jars so tightly shut, Tony expected the crack of breaking glass any minute.

"Okay, fine," she said. "At least we have that straight."

"Hold on." He reached for the basket lid just as a plate landed on his knuckles. Wincing, he waited until she got her trembling chin under control.

She forced her clamped lips into a dignified line. "I suppose it's really none of my business."

"Will you let me explain?" Another doozy from the world of cheating men. The plea landed like a dead duck.

"You can explain having groupies in your hotel room?"

"Yes."

"Holding them? Hugging them?"

"I was new to Chicago."

She waved a plate at him. Although he knew it was only a gesture, he ducked as she threw it Frisbee style into the basket. "You were lonely. I get the picture. I know what those women are after."

"Do you? No one's really looked at their side of the story."

"Until you came along."

Great move, Paretti, defend them. Tony tried again. "I wanted to get to know *them*, not the other way around."

"You got to know them all right. Seven days' worth of columns. I can read between the lines."

"Read what I wrote. They're not all sexual predators. Deep down they crave attention. They need to be noticed by figures of authority, celebrities."

"Did they get any attention from a certain celebrity sportswriter?"

"They didn't want it."

"Ooh, that must have hurt your pride."

"Don't sound so happy about it."

She'd found a tender spot, and like any good married woman, she prodded it unmercifully. "They weren't impressed with the prizes?"

"Who am I compared to Michael Jordan or Scottie Pippen? They aren't on the lookout for ink-stained wretches."

"But you could have made them famous in your column."

"The idea did intrigue a few of them."

She spun around to confront him, her eyes flaring. "So you did have offers!"

"I didn't say I took them up on it. The ones who wanted one more notch on their garter belts didn't interest me. It's the young ones who got to me, the teenagers. They'd believe any promise some high-on-himself athlete made. If a guy handed one his hotel key, she'd walk around glowing."

"And?"

He shrugged.

Sara hadn't been married to him for ten years without learning his little evasions. "Tony."

He looked up, more guilty than she wanted to see. "I took one or two of them to my room instead. Those guys weren't going to treat 'em right."

"One or two?"

"Just the teenage ones."

"I'm going to be sick."

"What did I say?"

She pressed her back to the wall, her hand clamped over her mouth.

"I didn't sleep with them. They were kids. Remember the Shauna character? She'd been hanging out with some creep who got cut from the third string of the Chicago Bears. Before checking out of the hotel, he took his frustration out on her. I saw her in the hall trying to hide her black eye and took her to my room."

"Whatever you say, don't say you 'just talked.' "

"We didn't."

Sara paled.

He took her hand. "I got some ice for her eye and held her until she stopped crying. Then we talked. She told me about the home life she'd run away from, the athletes she'd chased after—confusing attention with real affection. I bought her a plane ticket and sent her back to North Dakota."

"Why not a bus ticket?"

He shrugged, tilting his head at a rakish angle. "You know me and money."

She frowned, obviously struggling. "You always were generous to a fault."

"I didn't sleep with any of them. I figured they'd had enough of that." He waited, anxiously watching her set features, her compressed lips, her brimming eyes.

At last a tear leaked out. "Damn you."

His heart grew still. She hated him. "Sara."

She crumpled linens and napkins in her fists. "Damn, damn, damn you, Tony Paretti."

"You think I'm lying?"

She shook her head, dislodging another tear. "I knew it! It was right there in your column, in black and white. The caring, the anger, the way you defended them. You are such a soft touch. And such an honorable, sympathetic, predictable, irritating man!"

He got up on his knees. "Ten years, Sara. A hundred road trips. Not once was I unfaithful to you. Not then, not this past year."

"Never?"

He shook his head. "I sat in hotel rooms staring at the walls, wanting to pick up the phone and call the way I used to. I needed you, not substitutes."

"All you had to do was call."

They paused a long time, listening to the squeak of a passing elevator, the sudden swell of an old romantic standard on the hidden speakers. Sara looked up, seeking the source of the music. "One phone call. Do you think that's all we needed?"

"Never underestimate a lucky break."

"But it isn't luck. Marriages need to be worked at."

He would have said they needed to be lived, one day at a time, but he didn't want to point out another of their differences. "Then we'll work at it."

"But until we know where we went wrong in the past, we won't know if we—"

"—if we have a future?"

She laughed. "That's one of the great things about marriage. We can complete each other's sentences."

"Do I—"

"—do that? All the time." She sniffed. "Tell you what. Hand me my briefcase."

He reached into the corner. She shoved the picnic basket farther out of the way, organizing her space as a prelude to organizing her thoughts. "Clean the rest of this up while I make some notes. Then we'll talk."

Tony crammed jars and cheeses into the picnic basket, fumbling through the straw, rustling and rearranging. When Sara had their itinerary categorized and subheaded, she'd let him know.

His own strategy remained nebulous. Run-and-gun they'd call it in the NBA. Go with the flow, taking shots as they came. While she made lists, he'd bide his time, waiting for an opening.

He was still playing catchup ball, but he was getting closer. She was looking for unexplored problems that might have broken them up. To find them, they'd have to wade through all the happiness, the passionate nights, the close encounters. For every business trip he'd taken, there'd been thrilling homecomings, candlelit dinners left uneaten, a bedroom littered with mounds of tangled clothes and scattered pillows.

They'd been too happy to let it all slip away. She'd see that. And while she searched for the flaws, he'd be right there pointing out the irreplaceable joy. *I'm the only man for you, Sara Cohen,* he vowed. *Write that on your list.*

EIGHT

Sara frowned at her legal pad. "If we're going to do this right, we do it logically. Without anger or raised voices or out-of-control passion." She speared him with a look.

He looked as innocent as a newborn *bambino*. "Whatever you say, *cara*."

"We have to find out where we went wrong, or we'll never be able to go forward."

He nodded, licking the inside of the apricot jar lid before twisting it back on.

Sara wrinkled her nose, muttering to herself as she wrote. "First we list all the important dates."

Tony glanced over her shoulder at her cryptic abbreviations. "FD? ML?"

"First date. Making love."

"Put a star, an asterisk, and an exclamation point after that one."

Scribbling more notes, she poked the cap end of a

ballpoint pen into her curls. He glimpsed the writing her concentration produced, intense and tiny. Kind of like his Sara.

She talked as she wrote, naming topics. "Meeting the Families, The Wedding."

"Don't forget The Honeymoon."

She gave him a look. He gave her an unadulterated, sexy-as-sin grin.

She reached into her case and came out with a set of wire-rimmed reading glasses he teased her about every time she put them on. "We can start with meeting my parents," she announced.

"How about a quick review of ML?"

Her cheeks flushed. "You have a deeply filthy mind."

"And a supremely lovely wife." He kissed her on the nose.

She held very still, a disapproving glance magnified in two convex lenses. "Are we talking or playing?"

"Talking. But only under protest. You know me, I'd rather show than tell."

"Noted. We'll start with my parents."

"Hated me from the start."

"They didn't."

"They did. Eventually they grew to like me."

"Everybody does," she murmured.

"I like them too. Heidi and Abel just didn't think I was fit for their only daughter."

"They thought you were very nice. For a date."

"But not for a husband. So, do you think our ethnic backgrounds did us in?"

She exhaled slowly, thinking it through. "Ethnic, religious, social. We didn't have a lot in common."

"Except the greatest sex in the world."

Her lips thinned. "That subject is not up for discussion."

"It's up all right, just not for discussion."

She tapped her pencil against her pad.

He relented. "All kidding aside, your parents are great people."

"They're older. Intellectual. Not the most demonstrative people."

"Unlike my family."

Sara chuckled. "Your family are walking stereotypes."

"Effusive, emotional Italians."

"Maybe a big noisy Italian family and a small close-knit Jewish one were never meant to get along."

"They mixed like oil and water. Or mostaccioli and Mogen David. Cousin Vito the car mechanic and Uncle Moshe the rabbinical scholar only had so many things to talk about."

"Just so long as it wasn't Israel or the pope."

"Ah yes," Tony recalled, folding his hands over his abdomen. After one particularly voluble set-to in his mother's kitchen, he'd invented a whole list of imaginary sports their respective families might compete in when tempers ran high. "Lox flinging. The twenty-yard pasta toss. Bagel racing. Remember that?"

Sara chuckled. "I think their reading about it in your column shamed them into being a little more civil to each other."

"They've been on their best behavior lately."

Her pen scraped the paper as she underlined something. "Weren't they happy that you were finally free to find a good Catholic girl?"

"Nobody was happy when they saw the shape I was in."

She looked up. Every night of the last year seemed inked in around his deep-set eyes. "It wasn't easy for me either," she said.

He glanced at her list, as if realizing how close to the surface his pain had come. "Do you really think our families did us in?" he asked.

She shrugged, focusing on her legal pad. "My father thought I was infatuated with you."

"Were you?"

"Completely."

Tony felt the embers warm again. "You defended me to them the first time we met. Just the way you stood up for me against Melchior today."

He remembered that meeting as if it were this morning. No real reason he should, except that on one particular winter's morning a little more than eleven years ago, his entire life had depended on her parents liking him.

In the Upper West Side living room, Abel Cohen stroked his salt-and-pepper beard, studying the gangly young man with the curious job prospects.

"Sportswriting?" he asked, his faint accent conveying wonder, suspicion, and vague disbelief. "This is a profession?"

"Not like being a doctor," Sara said. "But it's an honorable way to make a living."

The elder Cohen's gaze made Tony feel as if he were under the Columbia University entomology professor's microscope. Any argument he made would be dissected, labeled, and pinned inside a glass case. Tony was Sara's college fling, Exhibit A.

"*Honorable,*" her father repeated. "*Defending those too poor for responsible legal representation, that's honorable. It's what my daughter intends to do with her life. Her mother and I wouldn't want anything to interfere with her studies.*"

"*I agree completely, sir.*"

"*Writing about ballplayers . . .*" He let the sentence hang.

Tony twisted slowly in the wind along with it.

Sara blushed. She and Tony both knew she'd skipped more classes in the last two months than she had in four years of college. Yet her grades hadn't suffered. Maybe Tony was right. Maybe life didn't have to be all work. All she knew for sure was that being with Tony made her happier and more confident than she'd ever been.

"*I love him,*" she said, her voice level and firm.

"*And I love your daughter with all my heart,*" Tony stated forcefully.

The Cohens shared a mild glance.

"*I won't pretend a sportswriting career will support us both in the manner to which Sara's accustomed,*" Tony said. "*She plans a career of her own, and I support her one hundred and ten percent.*"

"*Things are either one hundred percent or less,*" the professor corrected him. "*There is no such thing as—*"

"*It's a sports cliché, Father.*"

"*Ah.*"

Her parents traded another look. Classical music played from speakers hidden in the book-lined walls. Tony wanted to unbutton his collar or find a television hidden behind the paneled cabinetry running along the wall. If he and the professor could turn on a ball game and open a cold one, he might have a chance.

Silence reigned. The only words in the room were encased in a hundred closed volumes. Tony and Sara traded a look of their own. They're your parents, Tony's look said. It was up to Sara to break the news.

"We're thinking of getting married," she said at last.

Discreetly dismayed, Heidi Cohen was compelled to speak up. "Have you thought about this?"

"I assure you, if thinking had anything to do with it, I wouldn't get married."

Tony's brows shot up.

Sara gulped and sat up straighter. "What I meant is, I have a list."

"A list?" Abel, Heidi, and Tony spoke as one.

Sara grabbed her purse, digging out a yellow square of legal paper. "I admit we have our pluses and minuses," she said, scanning it, "but knowing what they are will help. I'm not doing this impulsively or without a great deal of forethought. I assure you of that."

"Well darling, that's fine, but—"

Tony interrupted. Enough polite chitchat. "I love your daughter. That's it. No list, no lie. I'll never hurt her. I'll look after her. I'll love her until the day I die. I promise you here and now, Professor Cohen, Mrs. Cohen, you won't ever regret she said yes."

Without so much as a glance in his direction, Heidi took her husband's hand.

He folded it in his, his lips pursed, his bushy gray brows furrowed. "Mixed marriages," he mused. "People might think—"

"I don't care what people think," Sara declared heatedly. "I love him. That's what marriage is."

Mrs. Cohen reached across the coffee table. "Be happy."

"If any couple can be ordered to be so," the professor added dryly.

"Abel, don't split hairs," Mrs. Cohen teased.

"You be good to her or else," Professor Cohen ordered Tony.

"I will, sir. You can count on that."

In the elevator Tony repeated the words to Sara. "Your parents surprised me."

"They surprised me. Twenty years of my life and I thought I knew exactly what they'd say."

"Maybe the list did it," he teased softly.

She crooked a corner of her mouth in a rueful smile. "Just goes to show you how little you know people."

"Even after years of loving them?"

His careful tone caught her attention. "I guess you can't take anyone for granted."

He shook his head, retreating to the subject at hand. "Maybe the love did it," he said.

Sara agreed. "They may be fairly sedate, but they are devoted to each other."

"And to you."

She shrugged that off, characteristically modest. "I'm their only daughter."

"I wish my father had met you."

Sara held out her hand. He took it with no more urging. "You've missed him a long time," she said softly.

"I was in grade school—"

Sara knew the story. Tony's father's death in an industrial accident had haunted him all his life. He'd told her how his love of sports derived from memories of his father: throwing a ball in the backyard, sitting on the sofa arm while his father and his uncles watched sports in the crowded den.

Maybe that's why Tony's whole philosophy revolved around good times and cherished moments. The people one loved could be taken away so fast.

After a quiet moment Sara looked for a way to bring him back from his memories. She picked up the pad where it had slipped off her lap. "Your mother is a great woman. She didn't care about our social differences or our careers."

Tony chuckled. "She cared about me being happy."

"And me being skinny."

"She was easier to meet than your parents."

"Easy?" Sara begged to differ. "I felt like I was walking into a living, breathing, shouting version of *The Godfather* parts one, two, and three."

Mrs. Paretti waddled down a hallway dark with flecked wallpaper. A lightning streak of white highlighted her jet-black hair. A black dress swathed her ample figure. Arms extended, she clutched her son to her as if he'd been gone for years instead of days. "Tony! Everybody! Tony's here!"

"Ma, I've got someone for you to meet." Tony gripped Sara's hand, pulling her forward while simultaneously tossing her an apologetic look. He'd warned her beforehand his accent would thicken like spaghetti sauce the minute they walked in the door. "Her name's Sara."

"What a beautiful name. Rhymes with cara. *And you, my no-good son—" Tony's mother patted his cheek,*

waiting to be charmed and knowing she wouldn't be disappointed. "What are you doing with a wonderful girl like this? Who are her parents, allowing her to go around with a heartbreaker like you?"

Tony ducked his head. "Ma, behave here. I want to make a good impression."

"And you expect me to play along? Tell her what a steady responsible person you are? If she doesn't know better by now, she will soon. Am I right, Sara? I see it in your eyes. She's laughing at you already, Antonio. This one's got a good head on her shoulders. But so thin!"

With an arm around Sara's waist, Mrs. Paretti never stopped talking. She led Sara past a formal living room dotted with lampshades coated by protective plastic, past a den filled with shrieking children playing an equally loud video game, straight into a bustling kitchen cramped with adults, shouted conversations, the mouth-watering aroma of dinner simmering on the stove, and a poker game in heated progress.

"Everybody!" she announced to the din. "This is Tony's new girl."

Hellos all around competed with the click of poker chips hitting the pile.

Mrs. Paretti quoted her son, a teasing twinkle in her eye. " 'Behave,' he says. 'Wants to make a good impression,' he says." She motioned Sara to take the last available seat. "Angie, get her a plate of dinner."

"Ma, she just got here," Tony said, wedging his way into the kitchen at last.

A shriek from the den made Sara jump. The indomitable Mrs. Paretti ignored it, dispelling cigar smoke with a wave of her hand, placing a plate of *heaping spaghetti before Sara, apologizing for the noise with a shrug and a tilt of her head.* "Ah, the children. Such noise but such love. You like children, Sara?"

Despite their gourmet sampler, Sara's stomach growled at the memory of Mrs. Paretti's dinners. "I thought I'd died and gone to Francis Ford Coppola's house."

"We can be a little overwhelming."

"We? There were thirty people in that kitchen. A nonstop poker game. Plates of spaghetti. We were there five minutes and your mother had a napkin tucked in my lap and a mound of food in front of me. 'Skinny girls have skinny children,' she said."

Tony laughed and quoted it with her. "So she was sizing you up for babies from day one. I told you that would happen. What's a family without lots more family to come?"

They chuckled together.

"I like your mother." Sara sighed. "Did she like me?"

"Instantly. She was afraid we'd overwhelmed you though."

Sara shrugged. "My parents insisted on speaking in complete sentences and actually listening when the other person spoke. Your family . . ." She let the observation trail off.

Tony turned his palms to the ceiling. "Conversation is like sauce, you throw everything in the pot and see what bubbles to the surface."

Sara laughed softly, her eye caught by the lock of black hair feathering across his forehead. Hesitating seemed silly. She'd combed that cowlick back a million times. She reached out then, holding it in place for a heartbeat. "They were one of the things I loved about you, you know. They don't hold back."

"Everything on the table. Food, cards, poker chips."

"Emotions, honesty, tempers. None of the long silences and quiet disappointments I sensed with my family."

"Your parents were never disappointed in you."

"I worked hard to make sure they weren't."

"*Cara.*" Only Tony could make a scowl sound like an endearment. "Your parents adore you."

"They don't show it."

"They didn't want you to get a swelled head. Look at me, the youngest son. I was spoiled rotten."

"You never doubted for a minute that you were loved."

"Or that I'd get sent to my room for a week if I acted up. No dinner. Cut out of the conversation. In my family, that's major trauma."

"I believe it." She nestled closer. "We're all so different."

"That doesn't mean we're incompatible."

Or irreconcilable? Sara wondered. "There had to be times you didn't understand me."

He thought a minute, struggling to put silence into words. "I never understood you when you got quiet. It drove me crazy when I couldn't talk to you."

"It was my way of dealing with anger. Withdrawing, thinking it out, never opening my mouth until I could express a disagreement in reasonable terms. Just like my parents."

"And I only got louder, trying to break through the wall you put up when you're upset."

"Your shouting did take a little getting used to."

"Did it break us up?"

"Oh no. We adjusted. You settled down."

"And you learned to speak up."

She raised her cheek from where it rested against his shoulder, giving him a no-kidding look. "I learned to yell."

" 'Yell' being a four-letter word where you come from." He touched her cheek, bringing her ear to his chest, letting her listen to the rumble of his laughter. "I was never so proud of you as the day you threw that pan of scrambled eggs at my head."

"Tony!" She pulled away, shocked.

He pointed to the door, a faraway look in his eyes as if describing Reggie Jackson's third home run in the World Series. "You didn't think about where to aim or what kind of stain we'd have to clean up; I said something dumb and you let fly."

She blushed, as abashed at the recollection as the actual event. "I didn't do it often."

"Good thing. Our first couple of years we couldn't have afforded the plates."

"I can't even remember what we were arguing about."

"That was the beauty of it." He turned her chin until she faced him, eager for her to understand. "It was pure emotion. No analysis. No lists. You told me exactly what you felt. Just like in bed."

Her smile faltered. His faded into something else, an unflinching stare, boring deep, seeking out every secret she could never keep, finding the love she couldn't hide. His heart thumped unevenly, a track runner breaking stride when he hit the tape. He moistened his lips with a sweep of his tongue, relishing the wine-sweet aftertaste of memories.

They'd been too happy to let it slip away. "What problems did we ever have that couldn't be solved? We never went to bed mad."

She nodded doubtfully.

"Look at the good things we had."

"But there must have been problems. Little things that led to bigger things. If we'd dealt with them then—"

Leave it to Sara to assume more analysis would solve things. Love solved things. "Whatever happened is over. Let's concentrate on what we have now."

She cast a wry glance around their lighted box. "A picnic basket, a couple of glasses of wine, and some discarded clothes."

"Sounds kind of romantic."

He watched her eyes darken. She hadn't meant it that way. As far as he was concerned, that's where everything led—to love.

He skimmed her upturned mouth with his, asking forgiveness whatever the sin.

"Tony—"

"Shh. This is too good to let go." He kissed her again.

Her fingers rose between them, tracing his lips, pressing him back. He kissed each of her fingertips, the space between them narrowing until her knuckles brushed her own lips. She drew her fingers away. He caught them in his hand, holding them to his chest, making her feel the relentless beat of his heart.

"We argued," she insisted breathlessly, grasping at the threads of their discussion before they completely escaped her whirling mind. "There must have been something—"

"Every time I blew up, I swore we'd never fight again."

She frowned slightly, lost in his eyes. "I wouldn't call it fighting exactly."

He brought her hand back, nipping at her pinkie. "Considering how we made up, we ought to call it foreplay."

NINE

He kissed her cheek so lightly, she leaned into him for more.

"This isn't a solution," she said.

"It worked before."

The marriage or his kisses? Sara's head spun, a slow delicious twirl like a lazy merry-go-round. Her lids felt heavy, her limbs boneless. She curled herself beneath his arm, the tip of her nose touching his neck. "Why did you marry me? I've always wondered."

A long-suffering sigh escaped him. She remembered it well—the sound of frustration whenever she wanted him to explain something he considered perfectly obvious.

"I told you," he said.

"When?"

"Every time we made love. I held you every chance I got. We made love a hundred different ways—and in almost as many different places. I thought you'd get the idea."

A flush heated her skin when she remembered some of the chances they'd taken. "That's showing, not telling."

"Actions speak louder than words."

"I want to know what you felt. Tell me."

Tapered male fingers reached for her list, tossing it off her lap to the floor. He thought for a second, but only a second, choosing spontaneity over circumspection. "I married you because I loved you. And I loved you because you had guts."

"Guts?" Her mellow mood lost some of its haze.

"You were brave, devoted, and loyal. And when it came to showing it in bed, you were totally uninhibited."

Vaguely disturbed, she reached for her pad. What if he'd fallen in love with a dream, some fantasy that wasn't her at all? "I'd never describe me as uninhibited."

"Once you're dedicated to a cause, you are."

Was she? He said it with such conviction, she nearly believed him. It was so typical of Tony. He made her believe in herself, supporting her in everything she did, urging her to take risks, then giving her all the credit when she succeeded. "Some of that was your doing," she demurred.

"Ours. You wanted the perfect marriage, and so did I. I fell in love with a woman who wouldn't give up once she set her sights on a goal."

They sat quiet a moment. With her head nestled against his shoulder, she didn't have to meet his eyes. She listened to his heartbeat instead. "Then what went wrong?"

"No," he insisted softly but forcefully. "Look at what went right. We were a good combination. We still are." He bent to catch her reaction. Her frown made his jaw clench. Obviously the answer didn't meet with her approval.

She adjusted her glasses on her nose and checked off the topics they'd discussed with a stroke of her pen. "If it wasn't the first date, and it wasn't the first time we made love—"

Tony leaned the back of his head against the walnut paneling. Who'd been fool enough to point out her persistence? He'd never deter her from finding the source of their problems. "If it wasn't meeting the families—"

"What about the wedding?" The next item on her list.

He ran a hand over the back of his neck, squinting into the past. Coaches would call it a question of attitude. He wanted her to see the good side of their married life, not some invented downside. "The wedding," he repeated.

"Everyone came."

"Except for our mothers sobbing in the front row, it came off without a hitch."

She added another check mark. "We got hitched."

He drew his finger down the air, scoring one for her pun.

Sara doodled a diamond beside the next topic. The facets shone light in all directions. Yet their steady progress through their early years hadn't uncovered a single insurmountable obstacle. They'd adjusted to each other's idiosyncracies like any other couple. Not a festering resentment to be found. So why did this sinking feeling gnaw at her? Because if they didn't find the answers in the past, that left only one agonizing issue unresolved.

The miscarriage. That's when their real problems began, the hurting, the blame, the withdrawals, the arguments that didn't get solved before bedtime.

But every time she spoke about the baby, Tony retreated, his eyes burning with a helpless, furious, trapped look she knew too well. He *wanted* to help, to heal their marriage. He just didn't want to talk about the one tragic, insurmountable event in their ten years together.

And she couldn't stay married to him if she couldn't talk to him. It was as simple and stark as that. "We have to talk about it, Tony."

"Sure. Next category." He tilted his chin toward her pad.

Her heart sank. Logic brought it up short. She couldn't automatically expect him to know what she meant. How could she expect him to know how she felt if she didn't say it?

But I said it a hundred times, her heart whispered. She'd said it until she'd driven him away.

"I need to talk to you about the baby."
"It's gone. Why can't we put it behind us?"
"It's not something you get over."
"We'll have another one."
"But what about this one?"
"What do you want me to do? I can't bring it back, Sara."
"You didn't want it as much as I did."
"I want to make you happy."
"Then listen to me."
"I'm trying!"

———◆———◆———

She closed her eyes, squelching the tears before they could fall, before he saw them and guessed their cause. He'd tried and tried. Until her crying drove him away.

But she had to cry. For the baby, for them. A thought drifted through her mind: He'd never grieved for the baby. Not the way she had. She'd never seen him cry.

She swallowed, fidgeting into a sitting position, her back firmly against the wall, the legal pad balanced on her knees. The issues were too thorny. They'd forced her and Tony into a corner—literally.

She sniffed and glanced around her.

"What are you thinking?"

She looked up at him, aching, lost, wanting to meet him halfway, unsure of where to start. "I was listening to that song."

He cocked his ear toward the ceiling, picking up the melody. "Criminal what elevator music can do to good rock and roll."

" 'It's the Same Old Song.' "

They studied each other, the barriers lowered for a moment. He wanted to heal their marriage as badly as she did, she was sure of it. Maybe it was time to focus on what they could fix and stop obsessing over things they couldn't.

She sighed and glanced down at her headings. "The wedding was as far as I got."

"How about the honeymoon?" He'd meant it as a natural next topic. It fell like a hand grenade between them.

The music turned to static, then went dead. Ten seconds of total silence ensued.

"We aren't talking about sex," she stated, keeping her tone rigorously cool.

"Did I say anything?"

All he had to do was look at her, and he knew it. "We aren't going to make love, Tony."

"So we talk about it," he said. He was so casual, he might have fooled her into thinking they could have a conversation about sex without falling into each other's arms.

That is, if her memory hadn't been every bit as keen as his. She'd never ever talked to him about sex without it descending into a demonstration. Or an exploration.

But he surprised her. He edged toward the side wall, keeping his hands entirely to himself. "We had a honeymoon."

"Most married people do."

"We have to look for problems there too."

"There weren't any problems there," she said firmly.

"I recall some sand in your bikini."

"That's hardly serious."

"We should be thorough."

"I'm thorough. You're the impulsive one, always caught up in the heat of the moment."

"Like the sun's heat in Hawaii? Or the temperature of satin sheets?"

"Tony."

"I remember waves lapping at the sunrise, lazily rolling from the horizon to the beach so they could stretch themselves at our feet."

"You're getting poetic again." And she grew more flushed with each receding wave.

"You wanted me to put it into words."

She'd wanted to move out of his arms and into

a world of analysis and diagrams—a world she felt comfortable in. Instead he gave her more memories, his words entering her mind like thieves, conjuring images she couldn't dispel, pictures that made her restless, yearning.

"Morning swims," he said. "Tides tugging at our bodies. The undertow swirling the sand around our feet."

Her feet pointed toward his. His leg pressed between her thighs. She knew undertows very well. They drew her toward something she'd been resisting all day, lulling her with memories of a happiness so pure, it made her ache. She compared those endless days of loving to the wounded, struggling love that had taken their place.

Her throat grew tight. She fought her way to the surface. "The next topic?"

"The honeymoon isn't over yet."

She shot him a glance.

He refused to meet it. Eyes closed, lashes casting black spikes on his cheekbones, he savored sultry images. "Remember us in the water, standing, me slipping off your bikini below the surface?"

All the important things happened below the surface, Sara thought. She bit her tongue to keep from saying it.

His words permeated her paper-thin resolve, sinking into her like water into sand, drawing her down into the memories they shared. A long-ago breeze hushed across her skin, warm as a man's breath, cool as perspiration. She folded her arms over her breasts, hiding the budded peaks, focusing a hazy gaze on brass doors that glowed like a Hawaiian sunset.

It wasn't fair. She'd asked him to keep his distance.

He had. She'd asked him not to kiss her. He wasn't. She'd scooted out of his arms, and he'd obligingly moved away.

She'd asked him to talk. Oh, how he talked.

He kissed her with words. He touched her with erotic impressions, setting flame to her fantasies. Sensations flowed through her like lava winding down a jungle path, pooling beside a waterfall. His memories linked with hers the way lovers' bodies did; two minds made one, sharing the same past, the same beaches, the same rumpled beds.

Her rebellious body supplied the reactions, her brain the agitation of waves. Resistance created nothing but friction. Events melted in a tropical blur.

"Hawaii," he said. Their one-word code. In ten years of marriage he'd lured her to their island over and over with nothing more than a word. He whispered it in her ear as the sun rose over Manhattan, reviving the rasp of sand on satin sheets. In a pelting bathtub shower, he'd prodded her thighs with his, rivulets racing down their skin in waterfalls of desire and memory. Hawaii.

In the elevator his voice sounded husky, sand scoured. "We made love in the open air. Remember?"

"That secluded beach."

"Not as secluded as this." He nodded to the four walls. "You'd dare anything then."

"With you to tempt me."

What if he tempted her here? Now? His crooked brow posed the question.

Sara pointed a finger at the opening in the ceiling, the one he'd covered with the flimsy tile. "They might come back."

"We'd hear them first. What's to stop us?"

She couldn't say. Words receded from her like the tide racing off the shore. She couldn't think, couldn't find the courage to look him in the eye. She knew full well what he'd see if she let her gaze meet his. She wanted him, them, all of it. She wanted it all back, to be in his arms and forget everything that had come between them.

But how long could she forget? How long before other, darker memories came back?

He crouched next to her, reaching for her cheek, brushing a wisp of hair away like grains of sand. She hoped to heaven her eyes conveyed the agony she felt. I can't do this, she wanted to cry. I can't pretend making love will make everything better.

"We have to talk." Her voice almost broke, the words ragged with repetition.

He slid her pen out from where she'd absentmindedly balanced it above her ear, caressing her earlobe with a fingertip. "So talk."

She stared instead, trying to gauge the depth of his hurt, to understand how something as simple and strong as their love could have gotten so tangled. "We were so happy."

"We can be again. Let it be, Sara. Let us be."

"But we have to find where we went wrong, or it'll happen all over again."

"Let me love you again. Let me show you what it was like. What still exists between us."

He touched her lips with his fingers. She gripped his hand, pressing her mouth to his palm. The taste of salt told her a tear had fallen. "Please," she said, begging him to let her go.

"I love you."

"Then help me with this." She knew he couldn't resist her plea.

He withdrew his hand, sinking back into the corner. With a twist he unbuttoned the second button of his shirt. Drawing up his knees, he balanced sinewy forearms on them, clasping one bony wrist with the opposite hand. "So, you tell me what went wrong."

She blinked at her list, the headings blurring with her unshed tears. In seconds they came into focus. She added a row of numbers, one through eight, the years of their marriage. Year Nine the baby had been conceived and died six months into the pregnancy. Year Ten, things fell apart. If they made it that far in their discussion, there'd be no more left to talk about. It would be over.

She coughed to clear her throat. "Year One."

"We were happy."

"Year Two."

"Happier still."

Annoyance crept into her shaky resolve. "You're not helping—"

"—to track down the bad things? We're on the brink of divorce, Princess. How much worse can it get?"

"There were faults we overlooked in the romance of the moment. There had to be. No marriage is perfect."

"Ours wasn't far off."

"Tony."

"Okay, money," he declared.

"Money?"

"We argued about it."

"It's the most common argument people have in their first year of marriage."

"Doesn't mean it didn't count. You said I over-tipped and bought too many souvenirs on the road."

"The plastic Elvis chapels?"

"The NCAA Quarterfinals, Las Vegas, Nevada. They don't call it March Madness for nothing."

"Each one had a tiny light that blinked on and off in time to a recording of 'Love Me Tender.' "

"Okay, they were tacky. The nieces and nephews loved them."

"And you certainly have enough of those." She actually laughed, shaking her head at the memory of eight delighted children and a house filled with the tinkling repetitive sounds of The King's first hit.

Tony fastened on her smile. He'd lost her for a moment there, lost her to memories he wasn't allowed to share. Now her eyes were bright and eager. She was organizing their lives in retrospect, structuring the messy, haphazard business of living day to day. "Next problem?" he suggested.

"Have we covered money, then?"

"Things were tight while you finished law school, but we were never in trouble."

"Until the building went co-op."

"Yeah!"

She glanced up, shocked. "You sound almost happy about it."

He was more than that. Elated, afire, he grinned at the memory. "You were a tiger. The minute we got that notice, you leapt into action. Organizing the tenants, filing briefs, injunctions, motions. For the first time I got to see the woman I'd really married."

She paled slightly. "I wasn't that bad, was I?"

"You were that good, Princess. The landlords never knew what hit 'em."

She reverted to doodling in the margins of her list, shyly pleased at the compliment. "I was only trying to protect our home."

"That's another thing I loved about you."

"I've seen too many people tossed out in the street because they didn't have the money to buy apartments they'd lived in all their lives. You weren't that bad with money. I just wanted to be sure we had some saved, in case it happened again."

"Always looking at the downside."

"People need to be prepared."

"With you to back me up, I felt pretty secure."

"Did you?"

Secure, blissful, content, settled, *married*. Watching his trembling Sara take on the landlords and their legal henchmen at a tenants' rights meeting had proved to him once and for all he'd found the perfect woman for him. He'd also realized that no matter how many witty columns he wrote, how many overpaid sports stars he interviewed, he'd never accomplish in a lifetime what she had in a couple weeks of research and case building. She saved people's homes. He entertained them over breakfast.

"What are you thinking?" she asked.

He plucked the crease in his slacks. "How proud I was of you. Intimidated too. As usual."

She waved that off, not even bothering to look up as she wagged her pen at him. "You always say that. There's absolutely nothing intimidating about me."

Oh yeah? She could leave him. She already had. The idea scared the hell out of him. Like a referee's whistle shrieking in his ear, the feeling of vulnerability stopped him in his tracks. He could search forever and never find her match.

"Anything else?" she asked blithely. "Year Two?"

"Your law finals."

"Did they cause a problem?"

"Aside from you studying night and day, no."

"You saw to it I took 'recreation' breaks." She scratched that one off. "You got the job at the *Daily News* that year."

"It meant a lot of travel."

"And a lot of homecomings."

He grinned.

She fought one to a standstill. "What about my cooking?"

"You know I love Chinese."

"But I don't cook Chinese food."

"Why bother when the Chinese restaurant on the corner does it so well?"

She despaired of her culinary efforts. "Mr. and Mrs. Sing practically adopted you. You'd do about anything to avoid my cooking, as I recall."

"I tried to help."

"By running the garbage disposal when I was out of the room?"

"Did I ever object to a single meal?"

"Does throwing up count?"

"You exaggerate."

"I can face it, Tony. I'm not cut out to be a cook. Besides, I had enough studying for the bar exam without adding cookbooks to the list."

"The problem was, you followed recipes as if they were formulas for rocket fuel."

"And you glanced at the ingredients, then flipped the book shut."

"Like any sensual pleasure, a meal can't be concocted from a manual."

"It didn't dent your manly pride to do the cooking? I didn't hurt your ego by making you family chef?"

He held up a palm, stopping her right there. "You cannot insult an Italian male by telling him he can cook. Uncle Michael makes the best pasta on the East Side, and Uncle Gino's marinara has been known to make grown men weep to be back in Sicily. Cooking and manhood are inextricably linked."

"Whew." She crossed that off the list. "I used to worry about that."

"You used to worry that if you weren't Superwife, everything would fall apart."

She peered unflinchingly at the fine blue lines. "It did, didn't it?"

"Sara."

She shrugged, intent on her diagram. "Work— Love—"

Tony held his breath, uncertain in what direction she was headed.

At last she found the words to say it. "Love is something people need to work at."

He gripped his wrist with his hand, the pulse pounding beneath his thumb. Breath eased out of him. They'd had this discussion before. "Love is a gift. You have mine. You never had to earn it."

"But if you take it for granted, it might dry up and blow away. If you say the wrong thing— Ask for too much—" *Mourn too long?*

She drew two parallel lines in the bent strands of carpeting, then erased them with her hand. "We lost it, Tony. It got away from us."

"Never." He clutched her shoulder in his hand, forcing her to look at him. "I never stopped loving you."

"You left."

"I thought you wanted me to."

She shook her head. "I couldn't talk to you anymore. You wouldn't talk to *me*."

Their problem in a nutshell, Tony thought, dropping his hand from her shoulder. He curved his free hand over a fist, kneading the tension into a tight knot. "It got so I couldn't say anything without feeling—I don't know. Wrong. Guilty. Callous. You looked at me as if—as if I were failing you."

"I needed you."

"I know it, dammit!"

She flinched. Tony bowed his head. The reverberation of his voice echoed in stark contrast to the filtered static their music had become.

"Don't you think I know that?" he said in an agonized whisper. He dragged a hand across his eyes, as if rubbing could erase the images they recalled. "Every time you said you needed me, I tried to be there for you. But everything I did came out wrong. Every offer I made, you turned me away."

Sara didn't know what to say. Shifting to the side, she bumped over a wineglass they'd forgotten to pack. She hurriedly scooped it up, watching a trickle of red wine slide down the inside. She tipped it to her lips, tasting the faint afterburn of alcohol. "I'm sorry."

"For what?"

"We weren't supposed to discuss that yet."

He laughed, a husky, dry sound. "Jumping ahead to Year Nine?"

"Let's keep this organized."

"Safer that way?"

She ground the tip of her pen into the pad, forming a big fat period. "I was hoping it'd keep us from falling into the same old ruts. Every time we talk about the baby, we fall into the same patterns."

"Such as?"

"Blame. Guilt. Need."

"You needed something I couldn't give."

"You tried."

"I tried to give you another baby. You just wanted me gone."

She gasped. "I never said that."

"You thought it. You didn't want another baby with me."

"I wanted to get over the grief of losing the first before we tried again. I told you that."

"How long? How long was it going to take to get over the grief?"

"I didn't know." But a part of her, a deep guilty corner of her soul, knew she'd used it as an excuse. The grief had subsided, bit by painful bit. But then fear took its place, the fear of what would happen if she lost another baby—and Tony refused to talk about that one too. She could have faced anything with him beside her. But not if he turned away.

Clutching the pen in her hand, Sara made a conscious effort to be fair. Tony had rushed to the hospital to be with her. In the months that followed, he'd pampered and held her every time she needed him. But he was reluctant to talk about it. The more she insisted, the more he withdrew. He went for long walks and longer business trips, anything not to hear her crying. He couldn't face it, he said.

And she couldn't face losing another baby alone.

In the elevator, Sara's tongue swept away the salty tear glazing her lips. "Let's work through everything else first. We have a lot of years to cover yet."

Tony studied her a long moment. Her face was flushed. She looked nervously to the floor, the doors, to Tony's grim expression. She tucked a curl over her ear and felt it fall right back into place, long enough to tickle her cheek, not long enough to hide her from his intense scrutiny.

"May we continue?" she asked.

"Next topic," he replied flatly.

She scanned the list, latching onto a sense of irritation. He made her feel as if *she* were the one avoiding the topic this time, seeking alternatives, distractions. "The And Game?"

"Ha." He raked the ceiling with a tolerant gaze.

She defended the system from sheer habit. "It was a good idea."

"Did I say anything?"

"What people *don't* say gets them in more trouble than what they do. The word 'and,' utilized regularly in a conversation, encourages people to elaborate. It was a system to keep the lines of communication open."

"You penciled it on the calendar once a month. As if you'd forget to talk to me otherwise."

"I inked it on the calendar. Talking is vital."

"I think we would've managed."

"It worked once you stopped laughing at it."

"On the contrary, *cara*. It worked once you *started* laughing. Moving our monthly conference to the bathtub did more to open our lines of communication than any system."

She recalled the way he'd combined her hyper-organization with the sinfully hedonistic pleasures of bubble bath and massage oils. The image of him singing the Mr. Bubble song while she tried to stick to a preprinted agenda made her laugh out loud.

That was her first mistake.

Letting him take her laughter as a cue to come nearer was a close second.

Getting lost in his eyes was her third.

TEN

His nose touched her neck and nuzzled there. "We burned those communication lines right up."

A laugh escaped her like a bubble bursting. "That is not communication."

"No?" He nipped her earlobe. "You know exactly what I'm getting at."

She did. Though every molecule in her brain protested, every cell in her body shuddered on the brink of surrender. "Stop that."

"And?"

"And pay attention. Year Three."

"And Four. And Five. Every year, you lightened up a little more. You began to act as if I'd love you no matter what. Which is what I thought I'd been saying all along." He repeated it with a wet kiss just beneath her ear.

She nearly crumbled. "Are you saying I was uptight?

I wasn't uptight; I was goal oriented. There were things I wanted to achieve."

"What if the goal is to enjoy life as it happens?"

"Hedonism was your department."

He proved it with a grazing kiss. "And my goal was moving your department closer to my department. Or at least a couple of your file cabinets."

"I wasn't that bad."

He backed off, a teasing glint in his eye. "What about your seven-year plan?"

"Are you saying my goals hurt our marriage?"

"I had a hard time seeing where I fit in with your perfect life plan."

"You?" She turned on him, bracing her palm against his chest. "Antonio Guiliano Paretti! How dare you!"

"Let's face it. What have I got to offer? You could have achieved everything you've achieved without me."

"Never! Don't you know you were the one thing missing from my carefully controlled, mapped-out, written-down, itemized, suffocating life? Without you I don't know what I'd have become."

He slipped his arm between her back and the wall, grappling with the effort it took to do something that was once so natural, seeking the courage it took to ask a simple question. "Why'd you marry *me*, then?"

"Because you were exactly what I wanted."

"You had a list?"

She scolded him with a scowl, her expression immediately softening. "I wanted more than my parents had. My marriage would be more than civilized decency and polite discourse. You were fresh air, a tornado of it. You were chaos and breaking eggs for omelets and whipping up whipped cream. You were exciting. And deep, deep down, you were decent and committed and tender and funny."

"And?"

She thought a moment. "And," she added softly, with just a touch of pride, "you were head over heels in love with me."

"So you believed me."

"Eventually." She smiled wryly, remembering incredibly earnest discussions over cappuccino as she tried to convince her never-say-die romantic that there was no such thing as love at first sight. He simply wouldn't be deterred. "You used to bring me flowers on Tuesdays because Tuesdays needed to be celebrated more."

"And you complained about the money I spent on them."

"And loved every last petal."

"You kept them in the vase until they were nothing but soggy stems."

"I couldn't bear to let them go."

"And here I thought you were a bad housekeeper."

She playfully punched his arm. "I kept them until they drooped, ordered you never to do that again—"

"—and I came home from my next road trip with another huge bouquet. Remember the ones I got you after you won your first case?"

Laughing, she sat back again, fitting neatly in the bend of his arm. "I got the Rodriguezes' eviction overturned."

"And I got you a horseshoe of roses."

She chuckled and slanted him a look. "It was so big, I thought it came from a Mafia funeral by mistake."

He laughed out loud.

"Seriously. I imagined some bereaved don's family receiving my tiny bouquet of sweetheart roses and starting some terrible turf war."

"They were all yours." He kissed her on the temple.

She closed her eyes, welcoming his embrace. Curving her arm around his back seemed only natural. "You snuck into court to hear me make final arguments in that case."

"After all the times you watched me at the keyboard filing a story, I wanted to see my wife in action."

"Jumping up when the verdict was read and yelling 'Yesss' is no way to impress a judge."

"I couldn't have been happier if you'd slam-dunked under Shaquille O'Neal's nose. My shy Sara, quaking in her stiletto heels in front of the judge. You were brilliant."

"I worked hard."

Only Tony knew how hard. In court she was calm, methodical, authoritative. She never ever got caught not knowing a fact or figure. With her clients she was a source of reassurance and steady strength, sturdier than some of the buildings they lived in.

But afterward, in the safety of their fourth-floor apartment, the real Sara came out, lively, intense, passionate about causes and people and him. Honest about her fears. When had she stopped confiding in him? He narrowed that down to the very year.

Not now, Tony thought angrily. Those conflicts could wait. She rested against him, relaxed, content. She belonged. A pang of joy pierced his heart like sunlight slanting into a dark room, and he held her a little tighter.

They both jumped when a blast of static erupted on the speakers, a phrase of melody followed by a sweep of violins.

"Think they've got this repaired?" she asked tentatively.

"Not yet."

She nodded, the crown of her head bumping his chin. He rested his chin there again as they waited out the end of the song. The elevator didn't move.

"What was this about my seven-year plan?" Sara said at last with mock belligerence.

"It was a great example of our personality differences. You planned our lives—"

"And you insisted we just live. Day to day."

"And night to night."

"Mm," she murmured. She lazily raised a hand, counting on her fingertips. "My plan was no more than common sense. Get married first. Then take a few years to get to know each other—"

"—make sure our careers were on solid ground—"

"—and the marriage too—"

"—before finally settling down to making babies. Year Seven."

"Right."

"Right."

She squinted up at him. "Are you making fun of me?"

"Only your plans." He scooted forward a couple of inches, aligning his hip with hers as they slouched more comfortably. "Believe it or not, we could have done all that without sketching it out on paper. People have babies all the time without planning to the month when to stop taking the birth control pills."

"Year Seven seemed very reasonable."

"My mother was pulling for Year One."

"That's your mother."

"And yours?"

" 'Whatever you think is best, dear,' " Sara quoted Heidi Cohen. She craned her neck to look up at Tony. "Did you want more spontaneity? Was that the problem?"

He thrust out his lower lip and thought a minute. "I wanted whatever made you happy. That's it. My single, solitary, lonely goal. If seven-year plans made you happy, seven-year plans it was."

"We did have fun," she said.

He couldn't resist that hopeful quality lighting up her eyes. "Oh yes." He gave the briefcase a discreet shove.

"And when it came time to have a baby, you didn't feel pressured or anything."

"Pressured?" He maneuvered himself closer, an arm around her waist, one finger toying with her skirt's waistband. "We'd always planned on having a baby."

"Or two."

"I'd have been happy however it worked out, you know that." *Loving you was all I ever wanted.*

"So we tried."

"Year Seven *and* Year Eight."

"People don't always get pregnant their first year." She'd read that in a manual. Once Sara decided to do something, she studied up.

Tony stroked her upraised knee, letting his hand glide a little farther up her thigh with each caress. The wool itched his palm; her heated skin warmed the cloth from within. "So, you think there were hidden disappointments in there somewhere? Lurking resentments?"

She shook her head. It stopped mid-shake as his hand grazed its way back over the mound of her knee and came in contact with her shin. Her lips parted. A ragged breath escaped. "What are you doing?"

"Remembering two wonderful years. Making babies."

She inched her ankle back as his fingers skimmed it. "Some people thought two years was two too long."

"My family, for instance?"

"Your mother kept giving me advice." She paused. "So did your readers."

Tony's hand stilled. If he'd been wearing a tie, he would've fiddled with the knot. He strenuously doubted one silly little column could have broken up their marriage. But they were too close to back off now. He was determined to do anything to win her back, up to and including talking about— "The column."

"Did you have to reveal to all of New York that we were trying to have a baby?"

"Think of the response it got." His voice practically cracked.

Hers got very precise. "Two thousand letters."

"Not counting postcards and telegrams." He moaned. "My editor thought I'd chase all my male readers away. They loved it too."

"They talked about it as if it were a sport! Sending in advice on scoring, touchdowns, goals."

"They don't call it re-creation for nothing."

She pinched his waist.

"Hey, I'm a sportswriter, not Ann Landers. What else are my readers going to write me about?"

"They acted as if getting pregnant were like improving a batting average or fixing a golf swing."

"According to the golfers I know, getting pregnant is easier."

Sara twisted around, the better to throw quotes at him. " 'Keep your head down'? 'Don't swing too soon'? 'Step back from the plate from time to time'?"

"Sports can be a great metaphor for life."

"If you're an arrested adolescent or a Pentagon general."

"Or a pregnant woman?" He waggled his eyebrows at her. "It worked, didn't it?"

She rolled her eyes, shuddering at the memory. "Did you *have* to announce we'd hit a home run?"

He laughed until the elevator rang with it. "That's exactly how I felt. As if I'd hit one right out of Yankee Stadium. Babe Ruth couldn't have done it better." He remembered to the minute the day that damn stick finally turned blue.

She came out of the bathroom with a resolute look on her face. So much to prepare for. So many books to read. There was a spare room to empty out, and paint, and paper.

Tony's heart nearly stopped as he lay on the bed, his legs tangled in rumpled sheets. He'd dimly heard her opening the flimsy cardboard box the pregnancy kit came in. It had been two weeks since—

He remembered the exact night the child would have been conceived. The wine they'd drunk. The dinner he'd brought home after covering a Yankee doubleheader. He even remembered the Yanks were three up in the American League East.

But when Sara came out of the bathroom, not elated, not teary, just ready, Tony knew it meant only one thing.

He leapt to his feet, nearly tumbling off the side of the bed. With one pounce he'd swept her into his arms, yelling and whirling her around.

"I haven't even said anything," she cried.

He waltzed her to a sudden stop and held her away from him, the better to peer into her eyes. "Well?"

His Sara could keep a secret for all of ten seconds. "Yes."

"Yesss! Yes, yes, yes!"

Three times, Tony thought. Three times for the three of them. He remembered that moment and all the ones that followed in a string of images. The clothes she bought. The colors she picked for the nursery. The lists she made. "You knew what school he'd attend three weeks after he was conceived," Tony said.

Her faraway smile turned wistful. "Who said it would be a he?"

"The ultrasound." He shrugged. "It would've been great either way."

She turned, fixing her stare on the mirrored walls. "I thought you didn't want to talk about it."

He nudged her a tiny bit closer. "We talked about losing it. Let's talk about making it."

She said nothing. He heard her muffled sniff, and his heart clenched. *Focus on the good.* "I'd never seen you so happy."

Sara wrestled with something she couldn't say, readjusting herself in his arms. "Those two years were wonderful. We had the same goal. We wanted the same things."

He gently turned her face to his. "We've got the same goal now—to stay married."

She shook her head, her lips trembling, her eyes pleading. "We can't pretend the miscarriage didn't happen."

Tony bit back his frustration. He knew this wouldn't come out sounding right, but he had to say it. "We can, just for a minute. Let's talk about beginnings instead of endings. We'll go back."

"How?"

He leaned forward, slow, deliberate, touching his lips to hers.

"Tony."

There was no rush. This is what it was all about, the best moments of their marriage, the joining, the intimacy, the fears and revelations. The great and glorious hope that their love would lead to a child. "We stopped looking forward when we got hung up on the past. That's when we got in trouble."

Her finely arched brows drew together as she searched for the words to argue.

He never gave her the chance. He kissed her again, the way he had on the front porch of her parents' house, before the judge at their City Hall wedding, on the first night of their honeymoon, and their last. All those nights. All those late-for-work mornings.

His tongue pressed between her lips. When he withdrew, he filled her mouth with more words, barely letting a breath of air come between them. "Remember what it was like to hope, Sara? To be starting out, aiming for something?"

"We can't—"

"Do you love me?"

She didn't say it.

He wouldn't make another move unless she did. "Do you?"

He expected his shy Sara to murmur it into his shirt collar. She pulled back instead. For an instant he caught her waist in his hands, afraid she'd retreat altogether. Instead she looked him in the eye, a resoluteness that bordered on defiance burning in her eyes. "I never stopped."

His heart swelled with a bittersweet ache. "Then we can start again. Remember it with me, Sara." He drew her downward, one hand beneath her knees, one arm behind her back. "Remember what we had."

She'd never forgotten. Not the taste of his mouth nor the feel of his body pressed to hers. He smelled like spicy aftershave, tangy and real. He smelled like the pillow she'd hung on to all these months, like a freshly ironed cotton shirt, the faint perspiration scent that was all man.

She recognized the war between gentleness and passion waging within him, the familiar intensity that burned in his eyes every time he made her his. Fear mingled with a curious excitement; her limbs quivered, and her pulse skated erratically through her veins. She knew what came next—and she wanted it every bit as much as he.

She flattened her hands against the broad planes of his back, pulling him to her, quaking at the power he held in such tenuous check. "Take me back, please." Back to a time when the hurts hadn't happened, when their love had been tangled only in each other, not the lacerating strands of a tragedy they couldn't escape.

They lay side by side in the elevator. Music resounded in fits and starts around them; it couldn't interrupt the unsteady pattern of their breathing. The elevator's carpeting was firm, not soft; durable, not sensuous. Where didn't matter. Being together was all that had ever counted.

Tony's arms curved around her, strong, sure. His clothes snatched at hers as they clung to each other. He kissed her again. She marveled at the reaction suffusing her soul. How many times had he kissed her as if he lived for her lips? How many times had he breathed the air she exhaled, dragging it in in hoarse gasps?

A thousand nights, her heart answered. Ten thousand. And each time had been fresh, new, astonishing. Each time they wiped the past away, riveted to the present. Maybe Tony was right; when she'd begun focusing on the past instead of their future, things had fallen apart. Maybe—

His teeth raked the side of her neck. He remembered how she adored that. She forgot everything else. Tony was all that mattered. Surrendering, conquering, joining. They'd done it all; it would never be enough. "I need you," she said with a moan.

His earthy chuckle sent rivulets of desire cascading through her. He knew she was his. His hand spanned her throat, gliding to the opening of her wraparound blouse, resting flat against her breastbone.

Her heart thundered there. Her breasts felt tender, too sensitive to touch. She stirred all the same, his thumb and his little finger skimming each mound.

"Open your eyes."

She tried. They fluttered shut when he closed his palm over one budded mound. Through sheer force of will, she opened them again. Tony bent over her, cupping her, stroking. Faraway bells of sensation pealed in the recesses of her body.

"I want you to remember," he said, his voice stark, his expression alternating between bleak desperation and ruthless determination.

Did he want her to recall their past or to fix this moment in her mind? She'd never forget any of it. He was part of her, always had been. And she'd hurt him terribly.

She caressed his face, the lean jaw, the deep-cut lines. The glimmering overhead lights threw his face into shadow, making him look suddenly haggard and lost.

Sara kissed him on the lips. "How could I ever forget?"

He tugged her blouse from her waistband, reaching around her to flick open the button on her skirt, stealing a second to caress her hip. She felt self-conscious, thinking for a moment of the five pounds she'd gained, knowing full well Tony wouldn't mind a bit.

But it had been so long. A year since— And that had ended in recrimination and loss.

Air shimmering across her breasts brought her back to the present. Eyes closed, she relished the sensation of his fingertips unfastening the front catch on her bra, baring her, tracing her, fondling and suckling until she caught her lip between her teeth. Then all sensations stopped. She realized he was looking. Tony loved to look at her.

She opened her eyes and met his. The emptiness of the elevator took her by surprise. For a moment she'd almost floated away to another world, distant beds, distant beaches.

But they hadn't escaped, not completely. Elevator walls hemmed them in. Lights glimmered overhead. Mirrors refracted empty mirrors, and the glow of a brass panel remained stuck on the number thirty-nine. They'd be rescued soon.

Wasn't this a form of rescue? Tony was trying to save them both, to snatch her from a grief she'd never been able to escape on her own.

"Take me," she whispered, arching into his touch, raising her breasts to brush the cotton of his shirt, holding him, moving for him when his hand found the zipper on the back of her skirt and it hissed downward.

Instincts honed over ten years told her what to do. She knew where to touch, what unspoken signals to send. He knew her utterly, good and bad, fragile and bold.

He wanted her bold now. The elevator tilted as he bent her back once more, filling her mouth with another potent, choking kiss. Then he straightened abruptly, bringing her with him. "Stand up."

She wordlessly obeyed. She tottered on her high-heeled shoes while he loosened her skirt with one subtle motion. It fell in a heap around her ankles. Her blouse hung open, her bra an empty web of lace. He hooked the straps with his thumbs, drawing blouse and bra back, gliding them down her shoulders. He bunched the fabric at her elbows, the better to haul her forward and claim her mouth one more time.

"No doubts," he rasped out. "No hesitations."

She replied with silent acquiescence, sinking against him, drowning in the depths of his kiss. Balancing against his chest, she used one toe to push down the strap of her shoe.

"Keep them on," he ordered hoarsely. "The nylons too."

A trickle of anticipation slithered through her.

He stepped back. For one numbing moment she caught sight of herself in the mirror. Her hair was a tussled riot of curls. Her lipstick was smudged, making her lips look even fuller than they were, even more kiss swollen. Her breasts were peaked by dark brown aureoles, budded so tightly, they ached for release.

But her partial nakedness was nothing compared to the way Tony raked her with his gaze. His eyes lingered on the garter belt she'd worn, black, trimmed with gauzy lace and one central rosebud of satin. Behind it her panties were demure pink silk. His savage look made her feel anything but demure.

He swallowed, licking dry lips as he reached out and touched that satin rosebud. She folded her arms across her bare waist.

Tony drew her wrists away. His gaze stroked her like a physical touch. His eyes followed the scalloped trim of the garter belt, the stark verticals of its black elastic, the fasteners themselves stretching smoky nylon in their intimate grip.

His fingers glanced over inches of bare skin at the top of her thighs, tweaking the elastic, releasing the snaps to slip her panties down. "Look at me," he said, sensing her tension.

"It's so—"

"Erotic?"

Maybe. But atop that skimpily clothed woman's body was the all-too-familiar face of bookish Sara Cohen. "You know I never thought of me as sexy."

A dangerous smile curved his lips. "Leave that to me."

He angled his hips forward, moving them in a devilish dance. "Look at *me*, *cara*. Concentrate on us." His mouth plundered hers, blocking out completely the view in the mirror.

She swayed, partner to his erotic tango. He thrust again, his masculinity pressed against her, thick and throbbing. She knew how he'd feel inside her, how tenderly he'd move, how expertly he'd take her down, diving into a whirlpool of blind desire.

She feverishly tried flicking open the buttons on his shirt, only to find his hand already there. Their fingers fumbled together. She raced ahead, searching for his belt buckle. His zipper was another matter. Her hand strayed to the shaft beside it, stroking him with an open palm, luxuriating in his indrawn breath, the tautness that invaded his entire body.

"I love you," she said.

ELEVEN

A raw moan tore from his throat. With one brutal move, he stripped off his shirt. A fine gold chain glowed around his neck, its gold cross glinting against his bronze skin. A wedding ring did the same on his left hand. His opened zipper revealed black boxers, short and satiny, the style he always wore because he liked the way they felt against his skin.

So did she.

He stalked toward her as she stood rooted to the spot. Pressing her back against the rail, he touched her shoulders to the cold glass, then lifted her until her hips balanced on chilly brass. "Put your legs around me."

Her cheek sank onto his shoulder as he stood with her, his bared manhood rubbing the inside of her thigh. The people in the mirror swayed. The steamy outline of a palm formed against the glass as he braced himself and steadied her.

She'd never watched him seduce her, never witnessed his drawing her into the maelstrom. Was it the newness or the familiarity that made her tremble with excitement? It had been so long.

Yet he knew so much. He could take her anywhere, explode within her like a star or leave her drifting on a lonely ocean. A door slammed somewhere in her memory.

She closed her eyes tight, opening that door, rushing after him down the hallway. Reality intruded. His shoulder muscles strained against her clutching hands; his body trembled for hers. The woman in the mirror wound herself around the man she loved, opening to him.

Tony circled her waist in a powerful embrace. He pressed inside as she tightened around him, against him. Lifting her slightly, he withdrew to his tip. With one rending thrust he brought her down on him.

A throaty cry tore from her. "Tony!" The elevator lights danced, mirrored images wavering and multiplying.

"Move with me."

She tightened her legs around him. Emotions cascaded through the images, unexpected tenderness, unexplored need. Regret met license, unspeakable freedom and irreparable sorrow linked. There was so much she couldn't say, so much their bodies had to say for them, imperfect, inarticulate, but oh so wonderful. "Love me," she whispered.

He buried his face against her throat, holding on, raking her skin with a breath-stealing blend of skill and knowing passion.

He carried her back to the rail, the shock of cold brass making her clench around him as he balanced her there. She quaked in his embrace, caught between the stunning contrast of cold ungiving glass and his hot rippling body. She ranged her hands over his chest, naked and slick. His arm muscles bunched when she grazed them, the hair on his forearms hissing beneath her palms.

She wanted him closer. He wanted to drive her wild. The rail was wide and round and just far enough from the wall for her to balance unaided. Tony used it, arching his body back, thrusting slow, deep and complete. His hands roved at will, bridging the distance between his torso and hers as he arced back again, moving his hips in a sinuous dance.

Sara groaned, begging him to close the distance. He did—in his fashion, hunching forward from his shoulders, leaning just close enough to kiss her breasts, to suckle and nip and tease.

She laughed in sheer delight, moaning in unrelieved rapture. With him she was open, unashamed and uninhibited. With him, and only him, she felt completely desired.

Tony grinned, laving her budded nipple with a stroke of his tongue. He loved her little "oh's" of surprise, every panted gasp. He knew when to touch, where, how long. He knew how to take her places she'd never ever been.

They mattered, didn't she see? They'd *made* their love. They could make it again. All they had to do was stay together. They were together now, united forever in the memories they made. "Look in the mirror," he commanded.

Restless, impatient, Sara writhed on the rail. Her eyelids fluttered, a troubled smile flitting across her lips. She moistened them with a sweep of her tongue. "Tony, please."

He planned to please her, thoroughly. He spanned her abdomen with his palm, stretching his thumb toward her sensitive nub. His chest swelled at the familiar sound of a gasp catching in her throat. Sensations threatened to drag him under as his body reacted to her building climax. He pleasured her until neither of them could bear it without exploding, then he drew his thumb away. He answered her mew of frustration by pressing softly on her abdomen with the flat of his hand. With a soft groan she begged for more.

Closer, he thought, they were getting so close. "Come with me," he whispered. "Stay with me."

He never expected a handful of words to open the floodgates. Emotions coursed through him, pounding in his blood. "I love you. *Cara*. I love you."

His chest pressed to hers. Her legs tightened around his waist. He felt the prod of a stiletto heel, the rasp of nylons weakly clinging to her legs. Her small white teeth dented her lower lip, biting, resisting. He thrust through her resistance, his body thrumming like a coiled spring. He drove again and again, losing himself, capturing Sara.

She cried his name. Spasms ricocheted through her. A buck, a shudder, a wild ride, he watched the reactions play across her face, thundering through her body.

At last she collapsed against him, her forehead dotted with perspiration, tendrils of hair clinging to her temples. Tony snuck his hand around her back, embracing her as she whispered his name over and over.

A tear trickled down his shoulder. He held her through those tremors too. He recognized these tears as release, emotions riding the crest of sensations.

She'd be fine. If he was lucky, if she accepted the love they'd just made, they'd both be fine. He felt a knot form in his chest as he waited for her next response. She'd said she loved him a moment ago. Was it strong enough to last? Would she come back to him?

Her chest rose and fell, heaving in two shuddering breaths. No longer hiding her tear-streaked face, she wiped it dry and looked up at him. A careless toss of her head chased an unwanted curl out of her eyes. She looked sultry and mussed and sexy as hell. He wanted to start all over again, to go back to the beginning. In a way, it's what they'd been doing all afternoon.

He kissed her damp cheek, tasting salt and skin. It took all his willpower not to be lured into the musky shampoo scent of her hair. "You taste almost as good as you smell."

She laughed, throaty and low. A flicker of doubt clouded her eyes for a moment. "Only with you, Tony."

She meant there had been no others. He believed her.

An aftershock trembled through her body, a spasm that made her hold her breath. Tony gritted his teeth. His own desire had yet to be consummated. He waited for a sign.

His wife reached up, heavy lidded, satiated, and knowingly stroked the vein on the side of his jaw, her fingertips caressing the curve of his ear. He wasn't the only one who knew how to drive someone wild. Gathering her tattered self-control, she took a slow breath that made her breasts rise. Her nipples skimmed his. She began to move.

Tony clenched his teeth, not in time to prevent her name escaping.

Eyes closed, she let her body decipher what her slow circular movements did to him. Her arms untwined, her fingers trailing the length of his corded neck. A faint questioning sound rumbled in her throat. Did he like this?

He'd die if she didn't stop it. "Sara, wait."

"Mm." A moue of disappointment, then a sassy "Uh-uh." Her eyes opened, her hips shifted. Her arms coiled around his neck with an iron grip.

He lifted her off the rail, stepping back to the center of the car.

"Do you want to watch?" she asked playfully, nodding toward the mirrors, never taking her eyes from his.

He'd burn in a hell of his own making for this, but he had to say it. "We've got to stop."

She chuckled low in her throat.

He gulped at how that felt lower down.

"We've got to stop meeting like this?" she asked saucily. "Making love in elevators *is* rather risky."

"It's probably illegal."

"I'll look it up," she murmured, her words muffled against the glistening, throbbing, strained-to-the-breaking-point cords of his neck. Her lips went in search of more trouble.

Tony braced himself. When she recrossed her ankles behind him, he knew this was his last chance. He thrust his hands beneath her armpits and raised her up.

She hovered at the end of his tip, her breath catching as she waited for the next thrust. "Yes."

Do it, his body begged. One final thrust and he'd brand her his.

Instead he lifted her off, all the way. He lowered her until she unwound her legs and placed two unsteady feet beneath her. If he let her ask why, let her look at him with those sultry sated eyes, he'd be sweeping her into his arms again, backing her to the wall.

So he wrapped his arms around her, hugging her so tight, neither breathed for a long moment. Finally he sagged against her, physically primed, emotionally spent.

"What is it?" Sara asked. "What's the matter?"

"We can't."

She waited for more of an answer than that.

Tony had forgotten that part of marriage. Being committed to each other for life meant every evasion eventually had to be answered for. A man could avoid an issue only so long. Better to be honest—it's what they were there for. "I thought it would be better this way."

"How?" She looked seriously worried and a trifle cheated.

"Sara, I don't want to make you pregnant. At least, not unless you want me to." He waited for her answer, praying for it to be the one he needed to hear.

Instead Sara thought before she spoke. She stepped out of his arms, her gaze darting from corner to corner, each one littered with discarded clothes.

Tony raked a hand through his hair and found it damp with perspiration. "Hell, we don't even know if we have a marriage yet. We can't be making lifetime commitments like kids. Can we?" *Can we, Sara?*

"No," she said after a long pause. "It was very wise of you to stop." She picked up her blouse, slipping her arms into the sleeves, wrapping it around her like a white bandage.

A disheveled and glowing woman in an unfastened garter belt and slightly sagging nylons became a sane and sedate attorney before his very eyes. Tony nearly laughed at the way she resumed her composure. The pain in his chest stopped him cold. He'd lost everything they'd just gained, and for what? Because he wanted to protect her? Because he wanted her to see what a mature, farsighted, priority-setting guy he was?

"I stopped because I thought it was the 'honorable' thing to do. As you said, there's more to marriage than sex."

"Oh."

He'd meant it as proof of his love. She didn't get it. Instead she hid her face from him as much as possible in a room with three mirrors. She bowed her head to refasten her garter belt, then bent to retrieve her skirt and step into it. The corner became her private dressing room, no visitors allowed.

"Talk to me," he said.

Zipping up the back of her skirt, fumbling with the button, she laughed slightly, her eyes catching his in the mirror and skating away. "Funny, this whole thing began because you refused to talk anymore."

Tony cursed, a harsh ugly word. He zipped up his pants and grabbed his shirt from a pile in the corner, shrugging into it, too flustered to bother with the buttons. He sat, letting the shirttails sweep the floor.

The cross and chain glinted in the light. He fingered the heated gold. The cross's edge cut into his palm. He was gut scared, waiting on the edge of an abyss for her order to jump. They'd get over this or they'd go down trying. "I'm ready to talk. Don't say it's too late."

Sara sighed and turned. She combed a handful of hair off her forehead with her fingers and held it back, staring in amazement at the scattered chaos on the floor. He wasn't any prize either, judging from the look on her face when she finally met his tortured gaze.

"What are you thinking?" he demanded.

She glanced at the floor. "That it was wonderful. You were."

"And?"

She stepped to her briefcase and pulled out her cosmetics case. "You said you loved me."

"I do. Love means protecting your partner."

"From another pregnancy?"

"I know you don't want another baby with me. Maybe I can even accept that—if it means getting you back."

Her hand closed around the end of her brush, the bristles poking into her palm. "You'd do that?"

"If you're afraid of what would happen if you got pregnant again, we'll see to it you don't get pregnant again. It's you I want, Sara, more than any baby."

She let the brush drop back into the zippered case, her hair too tangled to face just then. "Losing another baby wasn't what scared me."

"What was?"

She couldn't face him *or* her own reflection. She sat in the corner farthest from him, the words emerging haltingly. "I was afraid, if I lost another child, you wouldn't talk about that one either."

His voice rasped with frustration. "We talked."

"I talked. You listened, a little, then you tried to talk me out of it."

"I wanted you to get over it."

"I needed to mourn."

A tense silence fell between them.

"Then this is my fault," he concluded.

"I didn't say that." She struggled to keep the defensiveness out of her voice. When she spoke again, her tone was shaky but soft. "I think it might have been mine."

"How?"

"My obsessive need to talk about the baby drove you away. I was afraid it would, but I couldn't stop. I had to have someone to talk to, someone I loved and trusted. Instead I watched you get colder and more distant, the road trips got longer—"

"That was only at the end, when I'd given up trying to help. You wouldn't let me."

"Help isn't what I needed. I needed a shoulder, someone to hold me while I cried."

"I did that."

Yes, he had. She sensed his body tense even now as he remembered. "You held me as if I were a bundle of knives, Tony. As if it hurt to listen—"

"It did."

The words penetrated slowly, water seeping through cracks in a stone. Her own pain had swirled and swept around her so long, she hadn't seen his pain. *It hurt to listen*. She'd thought nothing could hurt more than turning for comfort to the man she loved and being turned away. But had she ever looked at his pain?

She focused on his anguished features, the memories etched in the lines beside his eyes. She held on to his revelation as if it were a branch in a swollen stream. She listened when he continued in a ragged whisper.

"I couldn't bear to hear you crying your heart out every night. The more you talked about it, the more helpless I felt."

"I'm sorry, Tony."

"For what?" He dragged the back of his hand across his mouth. "My incompetence? My callousness? Every time I tried to do something— Hell. The guilt didn't help either."

"Guilt?"

"I didn't know how to make it better."

He'd tried so hard, and she'd pushed him away every time. But some things a man couldn't fix. "You'd hold me for a little while, letting me cry it out. But then you'd tell me some awful joke, or suggest we get out of the house, or take a walk."

"I wanted to *do* something."

"And I wanted you to listen."

But the more she'd talked, the more she'd hurt him. Sara tried to make sense of it. The words whirled in her head. She stared at Tony across the trapped space.

He glared at the carpet, jabbing his finger at the gray flecks dotting it. "Talking just led us in circles."

"That's why I asked for the separation. I thought time apart would help us sort it out."

"Instead I took the bait and walked out."

"And when you moved away, I assumed you wanted a divorce."

"Are we ever going to find a way out of this?"

Sara twisted the wedding ring on her left hand. There'd been a time when it took more strength than she possessed to try again. A time when all the lists she drew up, all the pluses and minuses, refused to balance. For some reason that time seemed passed. A tiny glimmer of hope had begun burning in her breast, and the pain that used to overwhelm her when they argued remained at bay.

She linked her fingers tightly together, determined to hold on to the thread Tony had handed her. He'd been hurt too.

There had to be a compromise, a path between his turbulent emotions and her tangled logic. She groped her way down it, starting with the facts, moving gingerly into emotions. "I need to know I have someone to turn to, someone I can share my deepest feelings with. I want it to be you, Tony. I love you."

Her voice got small, tight. Tony's jaw clenched until it hurt. His stomach churned with acid. He felt like a blind man staggering through a forest. He kept reaching and reaching and never finding her. They could get past this, he knew they could. But how?

He groped toward a solution. "The bad things we tried digging up today, the disagreements, the clashes, the misunderstandings—"

"None of them broke us up."

"No, they didn't. We used to forgive each other. Naturally. Automatically." An iron band tightened around his chest. Misunderstandings, misconceptions, dead ends, there had to be a way out. "When your cooking was inedible, when I forgot to call from the road, when you could've read me the riot act over some trinket I spent way too much money for, you didn't. We got over things. We moved on."

"This isn't about a trinket."

"It's about our marriage. About making it work again. Sticking with it. We've both made mistakes, but marriage means getting over them together. It's the struggle that counts. It's what you get over together that makes a marriage strong. We can't let one thing break us up."

Her voice was crying-tight, her eyes glimmering with unshed tears. "It looks as if it has."

"Dammit, there's no manual on how to deal with losing a baby. We messed it up. We let it divide us. We can get past it. All we have to do is forgive each other and move on."

"Forgive each other for what?"

He swallowed hard. His persistent, incisive Sara couldn't just say yes. She had to examine every angle, dig through all the fine print. She'd zeroed in on his.

He gave it to her, chapter and verse. "Forgive me for not being able to give you what you needed. For being thoughtless and careless sometimes. For spending money we didn't have. For walking out like a coward the first chance you gave me, because it hurt too damn much to stay and watch everything we had come apart."

He'd said it all, except the worst part. The hell with it. There was no evading the truth, not at this late hour. If she wouldn't forgive him for what he was about to say, they might as well end it right here. "Above all, Sara, forgive me for not wanting the baby as much as you did."

TWELVE

"I don't believe that."

"It's the truth." Tony stared across at Sara, his head pounding, his groin aching from incompletion, and his heart all but shriveled. If he'd blown it, he might as well let it all out. "It's the reason I never wanted to talk about it. For fear the truth would come out."

She said nothing. Minutes passed. A whirring sound drew their attention to the ceiling. Engineer Scott's voice sounded on the intercom, disembodied and distorted. "This is an announcement for the passengers of Car Seven. The repairs are proceeding and should be completed in under an hour. Repeat—" The message repeated then clicked off. The rapid patter of a harpsichord sounded on the speakers.

Sara vaguely paid attention. There were more important things in life than the progress of Mr. Scott's repairs. For some reason Tony was trying to push her away—or distance himself from something that hurt too much to face. "You wanted the baby."

"Not the way you did."

"You loved it."

Tony shifted, his curved shoulders hunched into the corner, his hands dangling between his upraised knees. "I would have. When it was born. Until then, I cared about you more than anything. That hasn't changed."

Like a faint echo in the elevator shaft, Sara realized he'd tried to tell her this before. He loved her more than anything. At the time, she'd been too wrapped up in her own pain to listen.

Her breathing grew shallow and short. In the turmoil of their breakup, he'd felt things he'd never said, things she'd never asked him about, *assuming* he felt the grief and loss as keenly as she did. She realized with a resounding shock that she'd never come right out and asked him how *he* felt. "Tell me about it."

Considering the way he braced himself before saying it, she wasn't so sure she wanted to hear it.

He drew his shoulders back and squinted at the ceiling, manacling one wrist with his other hand. "I was in Tokyo when I got the word."

The day she went into premature labor. She remembered.

"I was researching a feature on Japanese baseball. I got a message slip with Heidi's name on it and the number of the hospital where they'd taken you. It said you were in trouble."

He ran his hand along the back of his neck, ducking the pain. " 'In trouble.' It was a fifteen-hour plane ride. All I prayed for, all the way, was that you'd be okay. I didn't think about the baby. There could be other babies. I just wanted you—"

When his voice choked up, he coughed into his

fist to hide it. Sara leaned toward him. A terse shake of his head kept her back. He glared at the floor in quiet fury. "It died and you lived. 'Please, God, don't let her die.' That was the deal."

She crossed her arms over her waist, hurting for his pain. "You didn't kill it, Tony."

He shook his head, knowing that on one level, unsure what to believe on all the others. "I killed something else, didn't I? Like your trust in me." What damage had he done by not having the courage, the faith, to confide his feelings to his wife?

He'd tortured himself for a year, avoiding telling her the truth. When she'd needed him, he'd held back, unworthy of sharing her pain, urging her to leave it behind so he wouldn't feel so damn guilty. Over time, her tears fell like accusations. He heard them every time she cried. *You don't feel this way. You didn't love it like I did.*

She'd never said the words. His conscience did that, putting a damning spin on every request she made, hounding him, jeering at his sorry attempts to relieve her pain.

"Listening's tough when you can't share someone's pain," he said.

"You shared it. I know you did."

"I tried not to. I put up barriers as thick as the retaining wall at Indy. All for fear of losing you if I told you the truth."

And yet, just a crack in the wall made him feel as if a boulder had been lifted from his chest. She was listening, the boulder rolling away. A looming emptiness took its place.

"People always bargain with God when they're afraid," Sara said softly.

"Don't make me any excuses. I know what that baby meant to you. The minute it was conceived, your life revolved around it. Mine just revolved around you."

Her smile rippled like a wave, threatening to break on a shore at any moment. "And for this I'm supposed to hate you."

"There are plenty of reasons if you look close enough."

"There always are. Without love. And forgiveness."

He brushed her quiet faith aside, numbering the evidence against him the way she might have in court. "I shouldn't have brought home wine the night it was conceived; maybe the alcohol caused some defect. I shouldn't have been out of the country when the miscarriage started; I could have gotten you to the hospital faster than your mother did. I should have done more, thought ahead, planned for things. The way you do."

She tossed him a disbelieving look. "That would have prevented it?"

"I was there, remember? I saw the plans you made."

"That's the way I am. That doesn't mean he meant more to me than to you. You must have pictured him too."

Tony shrugged. "I was too busy picturing you."

Yes, Sara remembered. He'd taken armfuls of photos: her at the window, her gently rounded silhouette showing through a nightgown; sitting in a fuzzy bathrobe making ecstatic faces over pickles and ice cream; unpacking boxes of baby clothes and baby books. He'd loved every moment of her pregnancy.

In the meantime there'd been the love they'd made, gentle, thorough, reminiscent love, celebrating what their love had created, waiting to see what their love would bring.

An idea strayed through Sara's mind like a wave racing across sand. She realized with a shock, her volatile, excitable, passionate Tony had expressed no emotions regarding their lost child. That's why she'd been so stunned and confused when he didn't understand her grief, so perplexed at his attempts to get them past it. He'd wept with her, yes, but had he ever wept on his own? Or had she used up all their tears?

Sara fought her way through the confusion and muddle they'd made of their marriage. She focused on Tony now, on the pain he'd never expressed because he'd been so busy taking care of *her*.

It was so typical of him to put her first to the exclusion of himself. And it was so unlike him to bury an emotion. How could she have failed to see—?

"You cried for months," he continued, "and I ran away rather than deal with it."

Had he? She didn't argue. Tony felt strongly about everything in life, including his own transgressions. And what about their baby? Had he felt so strongly about that that he'd run away rather than deal with losing it?

Sara tilted her head, chasing down the idea as it buzzed on the edge of her consciousness. The puzzle was about to fall into place. Tony claimed he hadn't grieved the way she had. He claimed he lacked her feelings for the baby. Sara didn't believe that for a New York minute.

Sara looked hard at the past, the numb, terrible days and nights after she first came home from the hospital. Had she ever asked how *he* felt? Had she really been that selfish? The last year had been her, her, her. Tony had focused so exclusively on her grief, he'd never dealt with his own.

But he never mentioned his feelings, her conscience argued in her defense.

Probably because you were such a basket case that he didn't want to burden you, her mind tartly replied. That would be typically Tony.

Sara covered her mouth with her hand, shaking her head at the mess they'd made. Love wasn't always pretty. Sometimes, out of protectiveness, or fear, or grief, people did selfish things—the way she had when she'd accepted all his caring without considering his hurts. Or the way he'd risked losing her rather than telling her the truth.

Or else he used guilt to help distance him from the pain. If he told himself he didn't care as much as she did, it might hurt less.

But his need for distance had unwittingly pushed her away. When she'd demanded closeness, he'd felt even guiltier for not being able to provide it. The spiral of false starts and misunderstandings dragged them both down.

She spoke softly. "You worked so hard to help me with my grief, you never dealt with your own, did you?"

He threw her a look, muttering something about softhearted women. "Would it change anything?"

Just everything. He'd loved the baby every bit as much as he'd loved her. She saw the confirmation in his eyes. He looked wrung out, exhausted, like a man who'd given up. His shoulders slumped. Just as he'd looked the day he hefted his suitcase and walked out, Sara thought. But no one was leaving yet. They'd barely begun.

She chose her words carefully, probing the pain, asking, not assuming. "Tell me about the baby."

"What about it?"

"What did you expect? What were *your* plans?" Like any good attorney, she knew the answer before she asked the question. He'd planned to support her every step of the way, that was all. That was everything.

Across from her, he downplayed his efforts, dredging up an old joke he'd used in the months before the miscarriage. "I planned to have the greatest case of sympathy pains any man ever suffered. They would've wheeled us into the delivery room on matching gurneys."

Sara chuckled. Warm memories washed over her. They'd had such hopes. She swallowed thickly and set her own grief aside, fragile as a glass sculpture. "What else did you plan?"

Tony slanted his head as he studied her, not knowing where this was leading. He assumed they were still playing the game of reliving happy times instead of sad. They were skirting way too close to the edge. This was dangerous territory. But it was the only territory they hadn't explored.

"My plan, if you can call it that, was to make sure you didn't forget to have fun along the way. I'd show up in Lamaze class when you needed me, be in the delivery room when you needed me. What else are husbands for? I'd already done the hard part."

She shot him a wry glance.

"I figured the baby would arrive somewhere around the due date, and we'd take it from there. Take life as it comes, *cara*."

So he'd always told her. While she'd feverishly planned, he'd loved every minute of her pregnancy. He'd brought her crackers when she felt sick, carried grocery sacks over five pounds, and run out at midnight to get her weird snacks, even though cravings, according to the book, weren't supposed to start for another couple of months.

"Cherish the moment. That's you," she murmured. "And cherish the baby when it's born." She sensed him withdraw subtly, the barriers sliding shut like elevator doors.

"We never got to that part," he said.

"That doesn't mean you never loved it."

"I never knew it."

"But you must have imagined him," she prodded.

"What if I did?" he snapped. "You saw him, Sara. You held him."

She sighed and sat back and simply let the pain come.

She'd held him in her arms after the delivery, knowing he was dead. His tiny body rested on the width of her arm. Her mother hovered beside her, assuring her Tony was on his way. Sara kissed the baby's forehead and whispered good-bye.

Tony arrived the next day, frantic to see her. He saw to all the details, a memorial service, a tiny casket. The hospital staff seemed surprised they'd wanted that much.

Arguing with a nurse behind a curtain, Tony's voice

had gotten dangerously tight. "*Just because it didn't live until its official birthday—*"

"*Of course there can be a service,*" the nurse replied in a soothing tone. "*In cases like this it's strictly up to the family.*"

"*As if babies who die at six months aren't babies to their families. It's our son—*" His voice had broken.

Abel Cohen ushered him outside into the hallway.

Sara drifted back to sleep, numbed by the drugs they'd given her, floating on the edges of a pain so immense, the word "empty" didn't begin to describe it. "Tony's here," she thought. "Tony will take care of it."

In the elevator, Sara welcomed the emptiness at last. It had been so long since she'd had the courage to face it, to remember the truth. She waited until her voice could be trusted to come out steady. "Maybe you didn't carry him for six months, or make notebooks full of plans, but he was *our* son. Yours, Tony, not only mine."

He finally knew where this was leading. The bleak look in his eyes told her so. He shook his head from side to side. "I can't, Sara."

"Tell me how you pictured him."

"I can't."

"We have to. We must. Remember the first few days in the hospital?"

"No."

"Tony!" Her sudden fury nailed him to the spot. "If we're going to save our marriage, we've got to talk about it."

"We talked."

"Never like this. It was always me, you taking care

of me. What about you, Tony? We've got to resolve this, remember the way it really was, no matter how much it hurts."

He ran his hand the length of his face, looking haggard and gaunt, pulling his mouth into a silent scream.

"For love's sake, Tony?"

A short bitter laugh took her aback. "Love got us into this."

"And love can get us out. Please."

He opened his eyes, their dark brown depths bottomless and bleak, full of the knowledge he'd failed her before. "What do you want from me?"

"Tell me how you imagined him. After the ultrasound, we knew he'd be a boy."

"You wanted to know. So you could make more plans."

Her heart swelled at his weak attempt to tease her. She nodded, urging him on. "Did you ever wish it was a girl?"

He stared at the mirrors over her head. The back of his head thumped against the wall. He seemed to welcome a tangible form of pain. "A girl would've reminded me of you. Hell, I probably would have locked her in the house until she was eighteen. And warned her about men like me."

"And? What else, Tony?"

He shrugged one shoulder, casting a sorry look to the doors trapping them. "Stuff. I pictured things. That's all."

"Such as?"

He clenched his jaw shut, but no matter how tightly he shut his eyes, he couldn't block the images shining there, the dreams he'd had for their child. It wasn't like him to plan ahead, to steal the glow of a moment by rehearsing it. But that hadn't stopped him from dreaming . . .

Sara touched his hand. He opened his eyes and she was there, pressing in beside him, holding his hand in hers, squeezing his fingers to let him know no matter how hard he held on, he wouldn't hurt her. After an eternity of silent struggle the words rasped out of him.

"Sometimes I'd stand in front of the bathroom mirror, wondering where we'd put this so-called bundle of joy when he invaded our apartment, and I'd see him, right beside me, a little boy of six or seven, standing next to me with his own toy razor, pretending to shave like Daddy did. I don't know where it came from. It was so real."

Sara nodded. He watched her fingers twine with his, so much braver than he was.

"Maybe it had something to do with losing my dad. I don't know. I imagined us playing baseball, me and him, the way I had with my dad. Vegging on the couch watching sports. Signing up for father-son games. I could have taken him to work with me, introduced him to all kinds of stars."

"He'd have been the envy of every little boy in the building."

A faraway look lit Tony's face, and a smile he wasn't aware of curved his lips. "I remember walking into Yankee Stadium on opening day. I pictured this little kid holding my hand, his eyes big as home plate as he looked at the bleachers, the scoreboard, the grass."

His voice stopped suddenly. He pulled his hand out of hers, the better to wrap his arm around her shoulders and hold her close. She felt his chin press down on the top of her head. Her hand flattened gently on his chest.

"I forgot what it was like," he whispered. "Talking to somebody you love. Talking about—everything."

"It gets easier."

"Does it?"

"No." She shook her head, ashamed of the empty platitude. It didn't get easier, sometimes it felt as if she were sliding into a black pit. But Tony was with her now. Between the two of them, they could pull each other out. "It still hurts. Maybe it always will."

"Then how do we get over it?"

She didn't know. She groped for answers herself. She only knew that together they stood a better chance.

Then Tony let go. He stood gingerly, like a man racked with pain. He paced, stopped, paced again. He faced the corner and its endlessly repeating mirrors, propping himself against one with an outstretched arm.

Sara ached for him. There were some things that had to be handled alone, no matter how much people loved you. And she realized for the first time how he must have hurt, watching her grieve and unable to do anything about it. "Tony?"

He shook his head roughly. She stayed where she was. He circled the elevator as if gathering his strength. Hands splayed on the rail, elbows locked, head bowed, he looked like a prizefighter hanging on to the ropes, battered by blows but too proud to fall down. "Why?" he asked, raw and shaken. "Why talk about this now?"

"You need to grieve."

"I feel like hell, dammit."

"I know," she replied softly.

"It—It wasn't even real. It was barely six months old—"

"He was real."

"He didn't even have a name."

"We should give him one."

"What?"

Scrambling to her knees, Sara sat back on her heels and looked up at Tony. "We agreed on the service and the casket."

"In the hospital."

"But in all the months that followed, we never agreed on a marker."

"You wouldn't talk about it."

She glanced at the hands clasped in her lap. "Somehow carving the words in stone seemed too final. Maybe it's time."

Tony swallowed as if it hurt, and turned away. "I can't kid about this, Sara."

"Kid about The Kid? That's what you called him, remember? 'What're we gonna call The Kid?' you'd say." She leaned forward, imploring him. "Let's call him *something*, Tony. Please."

He nodded and drew in a ragged breath, raking the walls with his gaze. After minutes of silence he spoke. "Joseph."

"Your father's name," she replied.

"Yeah."

She thought about it.

He turned around. "You don't like it?"

"Too Catholic."

He barked a short laugh. "Wonderful."

"We never got a chance to talk about names." She shrugged.

"We probably would've argued for weeks."

Her heart leapt at his wry tone. That was the Tony she knew, joking, rueful, resilient. She tried another name. "What about Joel?"

"Eh." He shrugged.

"You don't like it."

"I knew one once. Second grade. A bully and a creep."

"Okay," Sara murmured. The more he talked, the more her hopes grew from a glimmer to a laser to a rainbow of light. They could find their way through this, she knew they could. "Your turn."

"Peter? Paul?"

"My parents would roll over in their graves."

"They aren't dead."

"They would be if I named a son after the pope."

"Think our ethnic backgrounds are going to do us in at last?"

"Not if we keep trying."

He considered that a long time. His gaze flitted from her hair to her flushed cheeks to her wrinkled blouse. Her small hands were clenched in fists on her thighs. Her whole body inclined toward him, imploring him to play along.

She knew he couldn't resist giving her anything she wanted badly enough. More important, *he* knew it.

He tucked his shirttails into his pants and grudgingly buttoned a button. Grunting, he got down on his knees before her, taking her hands in his. He prodded her fists with his thumbs until they opened. Lifting them, he planted soft kisses on each palm.

She looked so damned beautiful, so hurt, so hopeful. She thought love could cure anything.

Even this, Sara? he wanted to ask.

Even this, her eyes answered.

His chest felt like shards of glass. Every breath, every memory cut through him, leaving his defenses in tatters and his wife hovering, gazing at him with such hope, he couldn't back out now. "After all that's happened, you want to play name games."

She glanced away. Another shard cut him, this one deserved. "Try, Tony."

He let his lips linger in her palm one more time, an apology she accepted. "Antonio's out. I didn't want him to think he'd have to be me when he grew up."

"So?"

"John? James? Joshua?"

"Joshua." She sat back on her heels, tasting the name as she said it, thought it, let it float in the air. "Would your mother say it was too Jewish?"

"Would yours say it was too Catholic? It was Jesus' original name."

"A bridge between cultures, then."

"For a baby who was never really born."

She squeezed his hands in hers and looked deep into his eyes. "His name was Joshua," she said. "And he was six months old—" Her throat filled with unexpected tears.

Tony hauled her into his arms, crushing her to him as they knelt. "His name was Joshua," he repeated.

"And now that we've given him a name, we can say, 'Good-bye, Joshua. We loved you very much. And we wanted you very much—' "

A sob broke from Tony.

Sara coiled her arms around his neck. "I'm sorry. I'm so sorry."

He reared back, combing her hair off her face with both hands, smearing her tears with his kisses. "I'm sorry, *cara*. I'm sorry it didn't work. I screwed up. It was all my fault."

"We both made mistakes. I was selfish—"

"You were hurting, dammit."

"So were you. And I never saw it." Her eyes blurred. Her cheeks stung with the salty dampness of her tears, mingling suddenly with his.

They didn't know why, didn't stop to ask. In seconds her blouse was open, his mouth pressed to her flesh. His hands grappled for something to hold on to. Sara helped him with his shirt, not thinking, not arguing. A raw need seized them both, shaking them with hunger, an all-consuming, all-forgiving desire to be one.

Tony stretched her beneath him on the floor, turning to her. They'd lose themselves in each other, forgiving everything, forgetting everything. Except the love they made.

THIRTEEN

Sara stood before the mirror.

"What is it?" Tony asked.

"I was just thinking."

The rough huskiness of his voice made her skin tremble. They'd made love, savagely, absolutely, losing themselves in a passion that transcended pain. A year of yearning had ignited; shared grief became sharing. The pain had burned off in an inferno of matching need.

While their fevered coming together receded in Sara's memory to a series of jagged images, the unbearably sweet afterimages remained. They hadn't even thought to use protection. She hadn't thought to ask. The way they'd lost themselves within each other made worrying about such things irrelevant. She'd wanted to concentrate on Tony, on the emotional consequences.

Moments later, in the sudden quiet that descended on the elevator, she wondered what the emotional consequences would be for her.

Tussled, shaky, she pulled herself together as best she could. She dabbed on lipstick, then drew her blouse around her shoulders. Peering into the mirror, she settled it this way and that, never getting it quite straight. "I think my blouse is broken."

Tony chuckled on the other side of the elevator, a sound somewhere between a growl and a purr. "Getting ravished in an elevator can do that to a woman's wardrobe."

Sara sighed, opening the blouse and wrapping it a second time. The flash of a lacy bra gave way to the tender buds of her nipples pressing against the fabric. Both reminded her of the firestorm of emotion they'd passed through. Had they found peace on the other side? She briefly glanced at Tony in the mirror.

Half dressed, he watched her slip into her skirt, his look frankly possessive.

She eluded it by picking up another item of clothing. Quivery climaxes skimmed through her veins as she rolled up her nylons.

Tony cleared his throat. "That was really something."

But was it enough? Her trembling hands fumbled with the catches on her garter belt. Everything was so new, so fragile. Maybe they'd laid the past to rest, but they'd made no plans for the future. She desperately wanted to ask 'What next?' but feared he'd tease her for making an itinerary for their lives. For some reason she couldn't bear teasing just then. She needed to know.

"Sara?"

She turned back to the mirror as he stepped toward her. If she looked at him, she'd be in his arms again. She'd be begging him to tell her where they went from here, to make promises.

His hands closed around her shoulders, his long fingers kneading her collarbone. He knew full well where her tension collected, and how to ease it. He loved her, he'd always loved her. Somehow, during her terrible grief, she'd lost sight of that. His touch said he'd never let her underestimate its power again.

She sagged against him, his chest supporting her back as his arms curved around her in a hug.

A tremulous sigh escaped her. "I was so blind, Tony."

"Crying can do that to a person. It's all right now."

She grasped his hand. They'd cried together. They'd made love as if their lives depended on it. Maybe it hadn't been wise or prudent or planned, but for the life of her she couldn't regret it. It wasn't easy protecting oneself from love, especially when her lover prided himself on loving her so utterly, so completely. One hundred and ten percent, as Tony would say.

His eyes fixed on hers in the mirror. "Is that a smile?" He dropped a scalding kiss on the side of her neck.

She sucked in a breath. "We really ought to get dressed."

"Why?"

She gave him a quelling glare. "I think you can figure that out."

"We're not done yet." A thick strand of midnight-black hair tumbled onto his forehead as he kissed her collarbone.

She trembled. She had a sinking feeling she'd never be able to talk him out of making love again, not if that's what he really wanted. And then? "Stop kissing me."

"Never. And Sara?"

"What," she breathed out on a sigh.

"Thank you."

The simple words froze time. She met his steady gaze in the mirror.

"Thank you for Joshua."

Instant tears threatened as quickly as summer storms. She whirled in his embrace, her arms banding around his neck. She kissed him long and hard, and he kissed her back. "Thank *you*."

Touching him came as naturally as breathing. Wanting him filled her soul with wonder. Her blood heated, her stomach dipped. It felt as if they were sinking, then floating. Back in his arms at last, she could have held on to him forever.

On tiptoe, balancing on one stiletto heel, Sara felt the room quiver around them. "I love you so much."

"And I love you."

The world moved as their lips met. Sara gasped and broke away. "The elevator!"

Tony's head whipped around as they stared at the control panel together. The numbers were blinking upward, forty, forty-one, forty-two. "We're moving."

"We're going to be rescued!"

Panic seized Sara first. She snatched up her other shoe, clambering around the elevator frantically collecting litter from the last four hours. A notepad, a pen, a slew of mismatched clothing.

Tony caught his sport coat as she hurled it at his head. Forty-six, forty-seven. He'd never get that damn tie knotted right. He wadded it into his pocket. Swinging around to the mirror, he slicked back his hair with both hands. Sara's scream almost gave him whiplash. "What now?"

Panties, a wispy scrap of pink silk cradled in her hand like a live grenade. Tony's gaze flew to the picnic basket.

Ping.

Michael Melchior wrung his hands. He settled his watch chain across his somewhat rounded middle and patted his belly in a reassuring gesture. Pulling a handkerchief from his side pocket, he wiped his damp forehead and slid the folded cloth inside his breast pocket. Hands at his sides, he tugged the hem of his suit coat and stood at attention.

Beside him twenty attorneys, secretaries, and paralegals huddled around the elevator doors in a loose semicircle. Roberto and DuWayne, hands shoved into their overalls, bobbed and peeked over people's heads. Richard Scott stepped alongside Melchior, grinning from ear to ear.

Melchior sent him back to the semicircle with a quirk of his head and a disapproving frown. *He*'d do all the talking. For all anyone knew, they were about to be faced with a grievous lawsuit of mammoth proportions. Diplomacy was of the utmost importance.

Ping.

The elevator hummed to a halt. The doors whispered open.

As she bent over to pick up her briefcase, Sara's cheeks were flushed, her grin crooked. Her eyes widened at the size of their audience. One vertebra at a time, she straightened. The briefcase hung limply in her left hand, along with a shoe whose strap had somehow gotten tangled in the handle.

Melchior dimly wondered if the lack of a shoe accounted for her off-balance appearance. All her pinstripes seemed aslant. The V of her wraparound blouse pointed toward her left hip. Of the two buttons on her suit coat, one had seized a buttonhole by displacing the rightful occupant. And yet, Sara Cohen was a vision of decorum compared to her companion.

Tony Paretti glared straight ahead. He hadn't bothered donning his sport coat, slinging it haphazardly over his arm. Inside his half-buttoned shirt, a gold chain glimmered against his deeply tanned skin. Although his belt was fastened, the tongue hadn't managed to find its way into any nearby belt loops. His slacks were creased in places no decent tailor would countenance.

At least he had both shoes on, Melchior noted with a sigh.

Tony reached for Sara's hand. She took it automatically. Melchior dabbed his upper lip with his handkerchief, not even aware he'd reached for it. "Sara," he croaked.

"Michael," she said. "Hello!"

The rest of the welcoming committee stared back in total silence.

"About time," Tony cracked, breaking the ice.

"Mistuh Paretti," Roberto called out. "Welcome to the fiftieth floor, mon. Long time no see."

Tony glanced over the heads of the crowd, a bouncing set of dreadlocks catching his eye. "Roberto. Good to see you. And DuWayne. Thanks for all your help."

The two men grinned and waved. Tony returned the favor by waving his sport coat in their direction. Sara shot him a panicky glance and clutched his hand tighter.

Melchior scuttled forward. "On behalf of Melchior, Kravitz, and Keene, I'd like to extend our most heartfelt welcome and sincerest apologi—"

"Save the bull." Gripping Sara's hand firmly in his, Tony made a move to shoulder past Melchior. He intended to march her right down this hallway to the firm's offices. There he'd demand a private office in which they could regroup before facing those divorce papers. He'd gotten a lot of questions answered in the last few hours, but the biggest one of all still hovered over their heads.

Sure, they'd talked, they'd even shed a few tears, but she hadn't said a thing about the future. And if there was one thing he knew about Sara, she always had a plan.

Unfortunately, she wasn't cooperating with his present scheme. When he stepped forward, she stood rooted to the center of the elevator.

"Everything will be okay," he told her.

Her wide eyes fastened on his, not the least bit certain. Was it him she feared?

Acid sliced through him. Trust took a long time to rebuild. Maybe she didn't trust him to continue to confide in her as he had in the elevator. Maybe she'd have to stick around and find out.

Or maybe his persistent, determined Sara would go right back to her original plan and sign those papers.

Gripping her hand, he tugged her toward the threshold. She hopped across the door slot, tottering on her lone high heel. Tony caught her in both arms, settling her on her uneven feet as best he could. It wasn't easy cupping her elbow, not when one of his hands clenched a size-five pair of pink satin undies.

She took a deep breath and turned to the waiting crowd. "Free at last, free at last—" A bubbly giggle stopped her in mid-sentence. Sara *never* giggled. She cast a mortified glance at Tony.

So the armor wasn't back in place, he thought with grim satisfaction. Her composure was as rumpled as her hair was mussed. A sheen of color peppered her cheeks, branded by his afternoon stubble. The kiss-swollen fullness of her lips, the fever in her eyes, were his business and his doing. He had to get her somewhere private, somewhere they could nail down the details of their renewed marriage before it all fell apart.

But Melchior scooted in between the crowd and them, blocking their only escape route. "As I was saying, welcome to Melchior, Kravitz, and Keene. I hope your unfortunate experience was less of a trauma than an, uh, adventure."

Tony pulled himself to his full height before the portly lawyer, glowering at the beads of perspiration on the man's head. "I've got only one thing to say to you, Melchior."

"Yes?" he gulped.

"The lady would like to use the bathroom."

He'd said the magic words. The crowd parted instantly, a dozen sympathetic secretaries swarming around Sara to escort her down the hallway. A couple of them darted looks over their shoulders as they went, casting envious glances at Tony.

Sara never turned around. He stared after her, waiting for a look, a sign.

"Mr. Paretti." A freckled redhead bustled forward, tucking a well-chewed pencil in his pocket protector. "I'm Richard Scott, the engineer. I'm so glad we were finally able to repair this baby. She's a grand old model from the days when this was the newest building in town, however—"

Tony glanced at the young man's extended hand and wished dearly he could shake it. But there was this little matter of Sara's underwear. . . A nod sufficed. "Good to meet you. Thanks for everything. Now if you don't mind—"

He shouldered his way into the crowd, keeping the top of Sara's head in sight until she disappeared around a corner. Another lawyer came up beside him, a plain-faced man with a plainspoken manner that seemed totally out of place compared to Melchior's officious attempts at charm.

"I'm Conner, and you look as if you need a place to stretch your legs. How about here?" He opened the first two doors they came to, revealing a high-ceilinged conference room. "Have a cup of coffee, some tea. The humidor is freshly stocked with cigars, the refrigerator with yogurt, snacks, etcetera. The bar is at your disposal. That door leads to a private bathroom. Give us a call when you're ready."

Soundproofed walls muffled the sound of the doors closing. Tony looked around, dropped his sport coat on one of the eight leather chairs lining the conference table, and sighed. He wanted to talk to Sara, to know whether they'd made any progress at all. Their hours in the elevator seemed far removed from these imposing, sedate, impressive offices.

In comparison, the man in the bathroom mirror wasn't much to look at. The bathroom itself was a study in subtle shades of off-white. Tony Paretti was the spitting image of a haggard and desperate man in sorry need of a shave. He didn't look like anybody's idea of a lover or a savior. He hadn't rescued Sara. Hadn't saved their marriage. From the look of him, he was just one of the rats who'd been trapped on her sinking ship.

"Well, the ship got towed to port. She's safe and sound and doesn't need you around anymore."

Melchior would see to that. The last sight Tony had glimpsed as the big doors closed behind him was Michael Melchior taking up guard outside the ladies' restroom. No doubt he'd have the papers ready and waiting when Sara emerged.

She'd have plenty of time to look in her own mirror, Tony thought. He squinted at the bright fluorescents, so much harsher than the rose-tinted mirrors in the elevator.

When Sara looked in these mirrors, would she see the woman he'd loved? All the love he'd made her remember? Or would she remember the mess he'd made of things after the baby died—and see all too clearly the mess he'd made of her?

Her eyes would be puffy from crying, her mouth smeared from kisses. Her clothes—Good Lord. Tony stared at the panties in his hand and laughed despite the pain. His composed, reliable, sensible Sara was striding through a penthouse law firm without her underwear. In better times the concept would have stimulated him no end.

As it stood, he didn't hold out much hope. As much as Sara professed to love his spontaneity, his passion, she was an organizer. She'd planned on divorcing him for six months. Before that, she'd asked for the separation.

"Yeah, yeah, you took her up on it," he argued with himself. Nonetheless, he couldn't stop fears from milling through his mind like a throng leaving a football stadium, jostling, shoving, tripping over each other in their haste to get out.

Did Sara still want out?

Tony buttoned his shirt properly and shrugged into his sport coat. Shoving the panties in his pocket, he found his wadded tie. He drew it around his neck like a noose.

A soft knock at the door. *He'd soon find out.*

A secretary stuck her head in, her voice modulated and low, the carefully controlled tones a funeral director might use. "Mr. Paretti? Could you follow me please?"

He knotted the tie all the way to his Adam's apple.

Sara sat in Melchior's office, her slender legs crossed, her skirt hem decorously hiding her knee. Her clothes were completely presentable, her expression bland and unreadable.

Tony's heart galloped at the sight of her. If only he could pull her into his arms, talk to her, touch her. He'd written a hundred columns on the excitement, the rush, the thrill of sports. But when it came to the most important moment of his life, the words dried up in his throat. He loved her more than anything in this world. If she didn't know it by now—

Another swift flash of memory came back to him. The song playing over the elevator speakers when it had lifted off at last, the melody filtering through his head for the last ten minutes, was an old soul tune they'd both loved—"If You Don't Know Me by Now."

"Sara?"

Melchior stood on the far side of his massive oak desk. He, too, looked like an undertaker in his black suit.

Fitting, Tony thought, thinking of the words "till death do us part." In a way, a death had parted them. Joshua's.

"I'm sure you know why we're here today," Melchior began.

"To unjoin this man and woman from holy matrimony," Tony said.

Sara stared straight ahead, running her fingers along the edge of Melchior's desk. Tony's jaw clenched. Nothing had changed. He'd been nuts to think one afternoon and a St. Jude medal would make any difference.

"Here are the papers." Melchior set them out.

Tony stared at them until the words blurred. He waited for a sign from Sara, a tear rolling down her flushed cheek, anything. "Well?" he asked. "Do we or don't we have something worth saving?"

Completely in control, she stood. Her heels stabbed the carpet as she took her stand before the desk. Splaying her left hand over the documents, she reached for the pen Melchior handed her. Her wrist rested on the dotted line.

"Sara." The sound scraped out of Tony.

She tick-tocked the pen back and forth like a clock's pendulum. "Yes, Tony?"

"Look at me." He'd shoved both hands in his coat pockets. Now he withdrew them, gripping her hands in his as he turned her toward him. A pink set of panties cushioned his grip.

Sara's eyes widened in horror, color flooding her cheeks. She gave him her all-too-familiar "you wouldn't dare" look.

He dared. He'd let everyone in this office know exactly how much she'd loved him only moments ago. A pile of paperwork couldn't change that.

A panicky corner of Sara's logical mind told her no one else in the room stood close enough to see the scrap of fabric hidden in his palm. That wouldn't stop Tony from waving it like a flag if he thought it would do any good. He wanted her back. She'd absolutely die if he used her panties to do it.

While she stared daggers at him, he calmly patted his temple with silk and wiped his forehead with a strip of lace. Then he dabbed his lips on a tiny rose appliqué, a quiet kiss their eyes shared. He finished by tucking the frothy garment in his breast pocket.

Sara let out a tightly controlled breath.

Tony plucked the corners upward from his pocket in a jaunty triangle.

A sigh hissed through her gritted teeth. She grudgingly admitted to herself that the pink silk almost matched his tie. That didn't alter the fact he was enjoying embarrassing her in public. Again. "This is blackmail," she whispered.

Tony didn't debate that. His cocky shrug silently reminded her all was fair in love and war. He petted his breast pocket, making sure she got the message.

Sara fumed. Whirling on her heel, she set pen to paper. "Two can play at this game."

"As long as those two are you and me."

"Do you have any idea how easily I could make you my ex?"

Tony shrugged, deliberately casual as his throat closed up, his heart cracking. "Sara—" He tried to reach her, to touch her—

Too late. Meticulously drawing a diagonal from one corner of the page to the other, she crossed the page with a flourish. "An X. Just like that."

Tony stared at the giant mark canceling the first page of their divorce decree. He gingerly touched the paper, crinkling a corner with his thumb and forefinger. With a shaking hand he dragged it open, revealing the second page of clauses. "Just like that, huh?"

Sara made another X, putting it in black and white. "Just like that, Paretti."

Tony turned the rest of the pages. She crossed out every one.

He sidled closer, blocking their small audience of lawyers and secretaries, bumping Sara's hip with his. "If getting rid of me is that easy," he murmured, "I guess I'd better behave myself."

Sara muttered out the side of her mouth. "If behaving had anything to do with it, I'd never have married you. Propriety is not one of your stronger points, Paretti."

"Like making love in elevators?"

She burned a glance through his breast pocket, emphasizing another transgression. Suddenly the world tilted on its axis. It seemed to be doing a lot of that these days, Sara thought dimly. Falling, rising, floating, righting itself again. And every time, Tony's lips seemed to be locked on hers, his arms holding her no matter what. She wondered if that was a crazy coincidence or if that was love at work.

He set her back on her feet. Her arms unwound from their hold on his neck, her heart thudded back to a seminormal beat, her mind raced. They had to get out of there. There were plans to be made, places to go. They'd go back to the apartment and talk. Odds were they'd make love again, watching the snow fall gently around them.

Sara blinked as a few of those flakes landed on her cheeks, teensy white shreds of a divorce decree Tony was happily reducing to confetti. He barked a laugh. She joined in, wrapping her arms around his waist as he whirled her through the room.

They stopped at the door. Sara caught her balance and tried to catch her breath. She cast an apologetic if somewhat dizzy look at their audience. "I guess the divorce is off."

"Humph," Michael replied.

Sara didn't particularly care. She turned to Tony, leveling him as sensible a look as she could muster. "I think we'd better go somewhere and make some plans."

He swooped down and planted another kiss on her tender lips, lingering this time. "I think we'd better go somewhere and make love."

"Mm," she replied, her vision growing fuzzy, her lids heavy.

"Ahem!"

Sara glanced around. "Michael. Are you still here?"

Tony guffawed.

She gave him a completely innocent look. "But I thought he'd gone."

"Right, Princess. We're the ones going. We're going home."

Home. The word reverberated through her, leaving ripples of unease in its wake. Their apartment was so filled with memories, painful, joyous, troubling.

"Sara?"

"I have to think a minute."

Tony looked worried.

Melchior looked furious. He was in the midst of saying something, although no one appeared to be giving him any notice. Sara tried to focus. Something about a telephone communication.

"—from the Sultan of Surama," he repeated. "Surama!"

Sara shook her head. The name barely penetrated.

"As you might recall," Melchior ground out through clenched teeth, "the Sultan owns three floors of this building. His private floors are the reason we weren't able to free you sooner from your unfortunate captivity."

"Unfortunate?" Sara purred.

"Unfortunate?" Tony reacted, folding her in his arms. "That elevator getting stuck was the best thing that ever happened to us."

"Aside from our meeting," Sara said sweetly, raising her face to his.

"And getting married," he replied.

"And fighting now and then."

"And making up. All the time."

"And making babies?"

Tony wiped the hair back from her face, cupping her cheek in his palm. "We can start again," he murmured. "As soon as we get home."

"The Sultan!" Melchior practically shrieked.

His oblivious guests tore their gazes from each other in slow motion. "What about him?" they asked in unison.

Melchior nearly yanked his watch from the end of its chain. "While trying to repair the elevator, the first thing we did was contact the Sultan's people. Despite perfectly justifiable security reasons for bricking over every elevator door with access to his floors save one, the Sultan felt partially responsible for your predicament. Therefore he asked me to relay his best wishes to you and offer you a suite of rooms for the rest of the weekend. I advised him you were in the process of divorcing, but he directed that you be informed nevertheless." Melchior glared at a crumpled pink message slip in his hand. "He said, and I quote, 'Time and love are two parts of the same continuum. Please let them know.'"

"He sounds very wise," Tony said.

"Mm-hm," Sara agreed.

"What do you think, darling?"

Sara beamed at Tony. It was exactly what they needed. Their apartment would have been too personal, too filled with memories, for any rational discussion. A place unhaunted by emotionally charged scenes was what they needed to discuss their future. A nice, neutral, dispassionate, third-party, nonpartisan kind of place.

FOURTEEN

Neutral? Dispassionate? Nonpartisan?

Sara stood in the doorway of the Sultan's suite. A wall of windows stretched from the twelve-foot ceilings, revealing a stunning view of Manhattan. Billowing curtains trailed to the floor, fluttering there in puddles of richly colored silks. The fire in the fireplace, the nest of brocaded pillows on the low-slung blue leather sofas, the bottle of uncorked wine, made it the most romantic room she'd ever seen.

"Like it?" Tony asked.

She gulped. "What's not to like?"

The Sultan's manservant, a smallish nut-colored man with a perfectly round bald head, bowed deeply and pointed out a few other amenities. He informed them the other suites on this floor were unoccupied at present, the Sultan and most of his wives being out of the country.

"Most?" Sara asked.

The manservant discreetly bowed his way out of the room.

Alone with Tony, Sara waded through the plush white carpet, inching her way toward the bedroom. "Why do I get the feeling we're closing in on the harem?" she whispered to Tony.

"Because we are."

Rounding the doorway, they gaped at a tent of silk gathered in the center of the ceiling. Its folds clothed the walls in a myriad of colors. Transparent lengths of off-white curtained the king-sized bed. Its satin coverlet glowed in the flickering light of candle-shaped fixtures. From somewhere music played.

Tony chuckled. "From an elevator to a layout worthy of Cleopatra. What do you bet the bathroom has gold fixtures shaped like swans?"

She should have taken the bet. In the clam-shaped sink, water poured from the mouths of gold dolphins. Intricate mosaics covered every surface. The walls swam with vines and pieced-together images of ripened fruit. The tub was a square pool, three feet deep, lined with hand-molded translucent blue tiles that looked wet to the touch.

Sara laughed out loud at the beauty and extravagance of it all. "I don't think we belong here."

Tony, busy turning a dolphin's tail off and on, crossed the room to her. He tipped her chin up with his finger. "We're together. That's where we'll always belong."

Her eyes skated from his. She sensed him stiffen. She hadn't meant to hurt him, she simply had to think. She gripped his hand in hers; they'd had enough misunderstandings. "We have so much to discuss. For a few hours, time stopped and it was just us. What happens in real life?"

Sara read the answer in his eyes. This *was* real.

"Enjoy the moment, *cara*."

"I know, I know. But you know me. I want to know what our goals are."

"Stay married. Love each other forever. What else is there?"

Apparently more, judging by the concerned look that met his answer.

"Tell you what, in real life you'd need a bath after a tough day like this." Tony twisted the bathtub's faucets, unleashing a pounding torrent of hot and cold water. It gave him an excuse to busy himself, to do something.

Sara recognized the tactic. Whenever he'd run her baths after a long day in court, he invariably joined her in them. Was that what he intended?

He hefted a fluffy towel from a warming rack and set it on the ledge surrounding the tub. He chose a bottle from the ranks of lotions and oils on the opposite ledge. Plucking at his slacks, he balanced one shoe on the tub's edge and tipped a bottle with a French label. A milky rope of rose-scented lotion uncoiled into the tub. Tony stared hard at the water. "Do you want me to stay or go?"

That he'd even think of leaving while she undressed made Sara's heart skip. They still hadn't regained the ease they'd once had. She studied his striking profile, the glittering black of his eyes. "Give me a moment," she asked.

He left without a word.

Tossing her clothes on every horizontal surface, Sara sank into the bubbles. "Okay, relax." Her body ignored her command. Her eyes kept straying to that closed door. What was he doing out there?

He needed space, she told herself. After their intense closeness in the elevator, they both needed time to sort things out.

She heard his footsteps in the outer room, an agitated striding pace. A time-out, she insisted, that's all it was. She used the respite to review everything they'd discussed.

Tony hadn't meant to shut her out when she lost the baby. He'd been trying to shut out his own pain, to distance himself from more hurt than he could handle.

And she forgave him for that. Really she did. What scared the daylights out of her was that he'd continue to associate that pain with her, that he'd distance himself from it by leaving her again. This time for good.

Like a defendant before a judge, her legal mind brought the facts ruthlessly before her. If he wanted distance, would he still be here? Wouldn't he have signed those papers and headed for the hills?

Perhaps. But if he really loved her, why wasn't he there?

He needed space.

"Space," she spat. She slapped the water with her open palm. She was fed up with separations. Being together was all that mattered. Tony knew that. If he'd forgotten in the commotion at the lawyer's office, she'd sure as heck tell him.

She rose from the tub. Water rushed down her skin in rivulets. The door swung open, and Tony stepped into the room. Sara unconsciously raised her arms to cover herself.

He refused to look away.

Ripples coursed through her, deep inside. She

recognized that possessive, unflinching stare.

He padded across the floor on bare feet, wearing nothing but the forest-green terry-cloth robe they'd found set out on the bed. A purple striped sash cinched his narrow waist. But not for long.

"Don't go," he said.

She sank back into the water, watching in helpless admiration as peeled the robe off his shoulders. He was a man completely at ease with his body, oblivious to its sculpted beauty or the exquisite proportions of his shoulders, his flat stomach, his heavy manhood.

He lifted one lean leg and stepped into the tub. The water rose, rippling at the underside of Sara's breasts. She quivered as if he'd touched her.

He sat back, stretching out his legs. She licked a faint oily sheen of rose-scented water from her damp lips. "This space is even smaller than the elevator," she noted, casting about for something to say.

"It's huge, for a bathtub. How's ours, by the way?"

"Lonely."

So, he'd noticed her anxiety about going back to the apartment. Perhaps that explained his troubled withdrawal. Perhaps it was time she laid it on the line. "Tony, the reason I wanted to come here instead of—"

He barked a laugh.

"Now what?" she asked with a slight huff.

He lowered his voice, imitating a corporation chairman. "Ladies and gentlemen, the reason I've called you here today . . ."

She grimaced. "That stuffy, huh?"

"I'll admit we've held a lot of meetings in bathtubs over the years."

"Your favorite place for communicating, as I recall."

"One of them." His knowing look caught her and held. "There are a lot of ways to communicate, Sara. I think we worked our way through quite a few today."

And? She forced herself to say it. "So why does it still feel unsettled?"

He shrugged and thought awhile, water running through his fingers like sand. "It started out a classic grudge match. I scored a few points; you scored a few. With the score tied and the momentum shifting, the game was called on account of darkness."

"Could you translate that from sport-speak?"

"We were rescued too soon. Hard to say who won."

"Or lost? We can both win, Tony."

"How?"

"I refused to sign the papers."

"I ripped them to shreds."

"And? What's next?"

He swept a handful of suds off the water's surface, studying the wavering outline of her body beneath it. "Turn around."

She hesitated, wanting answers but too unsure to read the ones in his eyes. She should have known they'd lie in his hands.

He dredged her washcloth from the bottom of the tub and softly scrubbed her back. He knew all the signals, when to rub or caress, massaging her shoulders with shrewd, experienced fingers. When he finished, body-warm handfuls of water cascaded across her skin. A kiss touched her shoulder blade. She inhaled sharply.

Tony eased her down, pressing lightly on her shoulders until the ends of her hair touched the surface of the water. "I'll hold you up."

She believed him. She trusted him. Surrendering all the way, she lay back, more relaxed and quietly joyful than she'd been in years. "Tony."

"Sh." He placed a folded towel on the tub's edge and guided her floating body to it, letting her head hold her there.

"Don't let me fall asleep," she murmured.

He rested the back of his neck against the opposite ledge, his foot nudging her elbow to tell her he was there. "Do you think I'd let you get away from me again?"

She opened her eyes and studied him a long moment. He'd rinsed his face with a splash of water. Ebony-black hair spiked his cheeks. He lounged before her, arms spread on the tub's edge, chest expanded. He looked like a disreputable Roman emperor reclining in his bath. He looked like the man she loved, steeling himself for her answer.

She said it simply, making sure once and for all that he understood. "I needed you so much after the baby died. I let everything revolve around me."

"And I let it happen. Helping you deal with the miscarriage was easier than facing it myself."

"Or so you thought."

"It happened without my realizing it. The only way to avoid dealing with it was to avoid you. I should have seen what it was doing to us." He dragged his fingers across the water, shattering the placid surface, breaking up his reflection.

They both waited, watching it quietly reform.

"I'm sorry, Princess."

"So am I."

"Is it over?"

"I don't think so." She took the cloth from the ledge, her eyes never leaving his as she slid forward. Her hands splayed across his chest, the water-soaked cloth clinging to his skin.

Groaning, Tony leaned back, giving himself over to her sensual explorations, letting her tell him she loved him all over again.

"You like that, huh?"

He grinned, peeking through slitted eyelids. "I love you, *cara*. You are one sexy woman."

"Am I?"

It had taken him years to convince her. If she'd forgotten, he'd have to prove it to her all over again. Or let her prove it to herself.

They'd have a lifetime to work at it. Or play.

She soaped his neck, letting her hand curve on the taut cords of his neck. Her little finger slipped out from behind the cloth to trail over the vein beneath his ear. Her palms stroked his shoulders, her fingertips dancing on his nipples, toying with the wiry coils of black hair swirled in suds.

She rinsed his chest with handfuls of water, presenting them like a cupped offering, liquid strands trickling through her fingers. He couldn't resist her when she looked at him with such frank yearning. But once upon a time she'd resisted him.

He didn't wonder when she read his thoughts. They'd been lovers a long, long time.

"Tony, I'm sorry I pushed you away in bed."

A cautious breath. Once more, so much rested on saying the right thing. "You didn't want to get pregnant. You were scared."

"I didn't feel we could move on until we'd worked through what happened."

"You didn't trust me."

"Tony—"

He cursed softly, cutting her off. "I deserved it. I wasn't there for you the first time. Who's to say I wouldn't bail out again?"

She shook her head, reaching for his face. "You never gave up on me. Never."

"I left town, dammit."

"But you came back. Or was that just to sign the papers in person?"

She had him there. He glimpsed that triumphant glint in her eye, the one she shared with a jury after shredding some poor witness's trumped-up story. She wasn't about to let him off the hook.

Tony grunted. "I wanted to see you again."

She languidly stretched her arms along the ledge. When she shrugged, her breasts broke the surface of the water, caressed by rippling waves. "So? You've seen me."

Tony gritted his teeth. "I had to talk to you too. Although, as you've pointed out more than once today, none of this would have happened if we'd talked it out in the first place."

"I'll save the 'I told you so.' "

"Thanks," he grumbled, not entirely sure he'd escaped it.

"You're welcome. So what's next?"

He tried it her way. "We could make some plans. Set some goals."

Her careless shrug gave nothing away. Beneath the surface, her feet nudged his knees, tapping at the gate.

His eyes riveted on hers, Tony parted his legs. Sara scooted forward, water sloshing against the tiles. She didn't notice. Her knees poked above the milky suds as her body came closer.

Playfully, then thoughtfully, she drew a fingernail the length of his mouth. "We could enjoy the moment too."

"We could," he croaked out.

"Marriage isn't an accumulation of good times or bad times. It's staying together."

"Together."

"Together," she repeated, a dreamy smile curving her lips.

He pulled her onto his lap. She weighed nothing in the water. The womanly curve of her hips rested against his up-drawn thighs.

"Do you know what tomorrow is?" she asked.

If she circled her hips like that one more time, he wouldn't know his own name. "January something," he muttered. At the end of the week, he'd be off to Denver to cover the Super Bowl. He'd have to mention that eventually. But first he intended to be one hundred and ten percent sure she knew this separation would be strictly temporary.

The past and future settled, he brought his mind back to the present. Her wet breast pebbled when he blew a slow stream of air across it. It tasted like rose petals.

She arched back, her body strung taut by the sensations bolting through her. After a second she drew in a jagged breath, her lips drawn to his. "What was I saying?"

He nipped her neck. "January."

"What was the date on the divorce papers?"

He laved her ear with a kiss, growling low in his throat. "I didn't even read 'em."

She pinched his thigh. "I was hoping you'd notice tomorrow was our anniversary."

Tony stopped cold. One of her breasts rested its sweet weight on his thumb as he did the math. "Our eleventh."

"Or our first. It could be the first anniversary of the rest of our marriage. I want to start again, Tony."

"No." He lifted her off his lap.

Sara sat back so heavily, water sloshed everywhere.

Stepping out of the tub, Tony turned and yanked her into a standing position. He roughly frisked her with a warmed towel, muttering the word 'no' beneath his breath with every swipe. When the first towel was damp, he threw it aside and grabbed another. Neither managed to stop her shivering.

Tony barely noticed. Ignoring her dripping feet, he scooped her out of the tub and carried her toward the bedroom. "We don't start over, Sara. We had our first time. And our wedding day. And our honeymoon."

"But Tony—"

He laid her on the bed, the satin coverlet roughly shoved aside. His body covered hers, one leg finding its way between two damp thighs, one hand touching her core, coaxing out honey and heat. He watched her moisten her lips, turbulent thoughts haunting her eyes.

As much as he'd rather love her until the sun came up, he had to put this into words. There'd be no mistaking what Sara needed ever again, or what he was prepared to give her.

"We were married ten years, *cara*. Most of them were magic, one of them was pure misery, and one of them we spent crazy and stubborn and too far apart. We aren't erasing anything and starting over. It's part of us, all of it, the good and the bad. From the arguments to the apologies to the damned divorce. We're married, Sara. I want it to stay that way."

Small white teeth pressed into her lower lip. "You mean that?"

His kiss guaranteed it.

Sara accepted his proposal, from the way his tongue entered her mouth to the way his lips wordlessly promised her everything under the sun. He treasured her, and she did everything she knew to pleasure him. There was no hurry. They knew each other intimately; they'd been married for a very long time. She intended to stay that way for the rest of their lives.

"Take me back," she whispered.

"Where?"

"The elevator. The tub. Hawaii. Any place where it's just the two of us."

"Here." His body pressed into hers.

She opened for him, undulating beneath each intimate caress, his throbbing manhood cleaving her to her soul.

"What if—"

Her trembling fingers stopped his lips. She understood his question. "If I get pregnant, we'll wait and see."

"But—"

"No, Tony. I love you. That's all that matters."

He lowered his mouth to hers. "I love you," he whispered harshly. "Whatever happens, Sara, don't ever forget it."

His lips skimmed hers, his body taut and thrumming. A sheen of perspiration glinted on his skin. "We're in this together."

"Forever."

She held him to her as they raced through the night, holding each other against the dark, promising each other the dawn.